Even at the breakfast table, Delilah is painfully aware of how isolated she has become.

After everyone settled in, Delilah jumped a bit when Paul clasped her hand in his until she realized they all had joined hands for prayer. She only wished she could be a part of something so special.

For now, she'd just pretend that she wasn't someone they'd taken in out of charity. She listened as Gideon spoke of his appreciation for all of their blessings and asked God to be with them during the day to come. It seemed strange that they'd think God, who was so big and busy, would be right beside each of them all day long. Perhaps it just feels that way because they have each other to care about.

Paul's hand swallowed hers. It almost made her feel dainty and feminine sitting next to him with her hand cocooned in his warm, work-roughened palm. She stifled a pang of regret when the prayer ended, and after a slight reassuring squeeze, he let go. She sat as an outsider once again amid morning chatter as everyone passed around platters of eggs and bread with the coffee.

KELLY EILEEN HAKE has loved reading her whole life, and as she grew older, she learned to express her beliefs through the written word. Currently, she is a senior in college working toward her BA in English. She intends to earn her Single Subject Credential so she can share her love of words with high school students! She likes to cook, take walks, go to college group activities at her church, and play with her two dogs: Skylar and Tuxedo. God Bless!

Taking a Chance

Kelly Eileen Hake

Heartsong Presents

To Mom, Dad, Grandma, and Grandpa, whose love of God and history spark my imagination and enrich my life!

A note from the author:
I love to hear from my readers! You may correspond with me by writing:

Kelly Eileen Hake
Author Relations
PO Box 719
Uhrichsville, OH 44683

ISBN 1-59310-195-3

TAKING A CHANCE

All of the characters and events in this book are fictitious. Any resemblance to actual persons, living or dead, or to actual events is purely coincidental.

All scripture quotations are taken from the King James Version of the Bible.

PRINTED IN THE U.S.A.

one

Reliable, California, early spring, 1872

"Stop your squawking, Dan. You know she's staying—just like the last two." Bryce brought up a good point, Paul reflected. The family did have a history of keeping unexpected females. Wonder who'll get hitched to this one.

"Dibs!" Apparently Logan's thoughts followed along the same line. All six brothers turned toward the window where the woman in question could be seen from a distance.

It was no mystery why Logan claimed her. No one could mistake the curves beneath her travel-worn clothes. Glorious hair, darker than midnight, gleamed as the soft waves captured the last rays of the setting sun—along with the interest of every man within a square mile. Paul almost wished she didn't have her back turned, so he could see her face. Almost.

"She's taller than you, Logan," Bryce contested. That wasn't exactly true, though her slender build did bring her closer to heaven than any other woman Paul had seen. That presented a welcome change. Paul always felt a little awkward around bitsy Miriam, and Alisa wasn't much better. He didn't see how Gideon, the only one of his brothers to top him in size, managed being married to the pretty pipsqueak. Even Logan, the youngest and smallest of them all, knocked her over the first time they met.

"Why's she here, Gideon?" Paul's question stopped the beginnings of a squabble. The heavy sigh that came before the response wasn't encouraging.

"She's in a fix." The enigmatic comment set off a new round of exclamations.

"With the law?" Logan bolted upright. "What'd she do?"

"And she knows Miriam?" Titus couldn't quite keep the incredulity from his tone.

"I'll bet she's expecting. I told you if we kept taking in strays we'd end up regretting it." This from Daniel, who hadn't quite gotten over the bitterness of losing his own wife, Hannah. Personally, Paul didn't see how anyone with a set of eyes could think that slim waistline concealed a baby.

"You hush. Even I know the difference 'tween ladies and strays." Bryce, who boasted the least social graces of them all, took a stand. At last, the clamor subsided, and they all stared expectantly at Gideon. He'd explain. Then they'd vote on whether or not the mysterious woman would stay.

&

Delilah Chadwick kept her back to the house, trying not to reveal how anxious she felt. *I don't have anywhere else to go if the men don't let me stay.*

"Don't worry, Delilah," Miriam said in a reassuring tone. "They're good men who'll make the right decision."

"Maybe the right decision is to say no. I don't want to be a burden, but I don't see how I can contribute to a place like this. . . ." Who could want more than the beauty of the surrounding land? Blue sky stretched on forever over the rich, solid earth beneath her feet. The well-crafted house and barn built near it promised a cozy haven—and a garden. She'd always wanted a garden.

But Papa chased other dreams. He'd gambled his way from town to town all the way across the country until they'd finally ended up in California. He'd always said they'd get some land of their own as soon as he won a big enough pot, but then he'd turn around and "invest" his winnings in another game. She'd come along to take care of him, but she'd failed miserably. *Oh, Papa. I miss you so much.*

Miriam's voice interrupted her reverie. "But there's plenty to do around here, I'll tell you that much! With the baby coming, I need more help than Alisa can provide. Cooking for and cleaning up after six men isn't as easy as you'd think!"

Delilah knew she could feel herself turning red. "Miriam, I—I can't cook. We never had a stove. . .and when we were on the go, we just ate hardtack and jerky." This would never work! If she could offer them nothing, she'd be sent packing. That's just how the world worked.

"That's all right. You'll learn soon enough. I'll enjoy teaching you. Besides, I wasn't finished yet." Miriam began ticking off chores. "There's still the washing and mending—enough to keep a small army busy—so your needle will be appreciated. Then there're the girls and the weeds in the garden, which both grow far too quickly if you ask me! Of course, we can't forget the livestock. Every day there are eggs to gather, chickens to feed, pigs to slop, and cows to milk—"

"All right! All right! I get your point. I'm a quick learner and a hard worker. You'll just have to teach me everything." Well, not everything. She already did laundry and mending. As a matter of fact, she handled a needle well. Maybe she'd finally have the chance to make a real quilt.

"Will they really let me stay, Miriam? They've been in there for a while."

"Oh, they're just being Chance men. Like I said, they'll make the right decision. And if they don't, they're in for it. They've always been staunchly democratic about making major decisions. They voted the same way about letting me and Alisa stay. But they're going to have to factor in the Chance women now. We've already weighed in on the subject. Right, Alisa?" Miriam tacked on as the only other Chance woman rejoined them. Alisa had just made a quick trip to check on Dan's girls, who were playing with their dollhouse in a cabin.

Alisa laughed. "That's right. If need be, we'll have our say, too." She sobered a bit and turned to Delilah. "How are you holding up?"

Delilah offered a halfhearted smile. "I've been better."

"I'm so sorry you lost your father."

Delilah tried to tamp down the tears that sprang to her eyes. She still couldn't believe they'd buried Papa earlier that week. But now he was gone, and she was all alone. There hadn't been very many options since she only owned her clothes and sketchpads. Very little money and some worthless stock Papa had won the night before were stashed in the false bottom of her valise, but they wouldn't get her very far, and only one profession opened to unclaimed women on the frontier.

The pot he'd had the winning hand for last night went to fund the burial, such as it was. She and the sheriff stood side by side, the only ones at the gravesite. The circuit preacher hadn't been in town, but that was all right, since Papa didn't hold with much religion. It seemed sort of fitting, because since Mama's death, it had only been her and Papa wherever they went—and occasionally the law when one of his games got too heated.

Some of the more spiteful townspeople had muttered that it was only fitting a gambler should meet such an end: shot in a saloon for cheating. Delilah knew Papa didn't cheat. While her father couldn't stop gambling away everything they owned, Delilah came to understand a long time ago that he couldn't really help it. He made promises he never kept, but he'd always meant to. He was a man of integrity in his own way, and he never cheated. *Maybe if he did, he'd've won more. . . .* The nasty thought crept by before she could stop it. She hadn't really been herself since she found out they'd let his murderer get away. Was there no justice?

Not for Papa, but maybe for me. The men began coming out of the house to issue her verdict. Six behemoths, but she had Miriam's word that they were all "good men." She believed it about Gideon, since her cousin had married him, but she maintained reservations about the rest. They all stood fairly tall, each boasting brown hair and eyes. As they came closer, she tried to gauge what their answers would be.

She'd already met Gideon but couldn't read his expression. As for the others, one gawked at her past all reason, one gave his attention to an ecstatic dog at his side, and another looked politely curious. None of these gave any indication of a warm welcome. The brother with flowers in his pocket absolutely radiated hostility. The incongruity would have struck her as funny, if she weren't so anxious. As things stood, his glare made the possibility that she'd be turned away far too likely.

That left only one man, but he was different. She'd endured men gawking, scowling, leering, or being disinterested before, but this man's gaze stayed steady. It wasn't openly assessing like the others, but his scrutiny somehow made her feel as though he could take her measure better than any of them. His glance didn't feel judgmental but was disconcerting, nevertheless. She wasn't sure what to make of him, which left her completely in the dark as to whether or not he'd have voted for her to stay. That meant she knew the opinion of only one brother, and that wasn't encouraging.

"Well?" Miriam's tone sounded both as a question and a warning.

All of them except the scowler grinned as Gideon pronounced, "She stays."

&.

Paul watched as Delilah let out the breath she probably didn't even know she'd been holding. The stunning creature's smile managed to be both gracious and grateful as she thanked them for their kindness. Delilah was a lovely temptress, indeed, but her eyes truly captivated him.

From a distance he'd thought them brown, but upon closer inspection, they were no mere brown. Amber. Golden, pure, sparkling amber is what came to mind. Not that a gal possessed any power over her eye color, but the beauty of it snagged him just the same. He got the impression eyes like that should be full of joy and mirth reflecting the beauty around them, but hers seemed deeper with some hurt that didn't let her smile reach them. He wondered what she'd look like when she put those heavy cares on the Lord.

He'd watched her since the moment he'd stepped out of the door, seen her size up each of his brothers. Obviously, she'd heard something of them from Miriam and was trying to label him and his brothers. Had it been his imagination, or had her glance lingered a bit on him?

He realized Gideon still spoke. "You haven't met most of us yet, so I'd better introduce my brothers. This one here is—"

"Titus, right?" Her soft interruption stunned them.

"Miriam, did you already point out who's who?" Logan demanded.

Miriam laughed. "None but Gideon!"

Delilah spoke again. "Miriam and I have been writing to each other for years. From the letters I managed to receive,

I've pieced together some things for myself. Even so, Titus gave himself away since he went straight to Alisa."

Logan nodded. "All right, which one am I?"

"You must be Logan, who I'm told is the most sociable and outgoing." Paul noted she showed the tact not to mention to the infatuated youth that he stood the shortest.

"That's pretty good, Miss Delilah. Now do him." Logan jerked a thumb in Bryce's direction.

"Well, I've been told one of you has a special way with animals, so since the dogs followed him, I'd have to name him as Bryce." She looked around for confirmation, and when they nodded, she turned to Dan. "You have to be Dan. The flower in your pocket is a dead giveaway you're a father." Again, she demonstrated enough prudence not to point out the ever-present scowl. The moment those spectacular eyes trained on Paul, a bolt of heat shot through him.

"So you must be Paul."

"She pegged every last one of us, Gideon. Even old Gus White down at the general store can't keep the older four of you straight, and he's seen us more'n once."

Dan's voice put a damper on things. "All right, so we know she's stayin', but *where* is she stayin'? Gideon and Miriam got the old bunkroom, and the two rooms connecting the old ranch house and my place each have a bachelor or two in 'em. Titus and Alisa are newlyweds with the latest cabin. Where's she gonna fit?" Obviously, he had worked himself into a temper.

Alisa tried to avert the coming storm with a gentle request. "The girls have their own room now, and so do you. Maybe for a while Delilah could share the old cabin with the girls and you could use their room?"

The scowl softened only slightly, but that was something. "I figured you all were fixin' to kick me outta my own house.

I won't leave my girls, you hear?"

"I won't take anyone's home from them. A man deserves his own place, and so do couples." Her voice caught as she went on. "And parents should never be separated from their children. If it's all right, I'll just bed down in the barn."

She'd hardly finished speaking her peace before the menfolk gave their collective opinion of that harebrained scheme. Miriam and Alisa didn't manage to get a word in edgewise.

Surprisingly, Bryce spoke up first. "That's fine enough for me when one of the animals is ailin', Miss Delilah, but it ain't fittin' for you."

"That'd be an insult to our hospitality," Titus protested.

Gideon rested on a flat, "No."

"Don't you listen to old Dan when he's sour." Logan shot Dan a heated look. "That's just his way."

Even Dan seemed taken aback. "I didn't mean that, miss. What kind of example would that be to my girls?"

Apparently, Delilah nursed a stubborn streak. "I've done it before, and I don't want to be a burden."

Miriam opened her mouth, but Paul beat her to the punch. "We appreciate how you don't want to put anybody out, miss, but you need to be close at hand. It's the only way you'll be able to help Miriam while she's in her condition. I'll bunk with Dan, and you'll take my room—it's closest to Miriam's."

She looked at him intently, and he had to remind himself to steadily meet her gaze instead of getting lost in it. After what seemed like an eternity, she slowly nodded.

"Well, if that's settled, I'll just take your things on in." Dan reached out a hand.

"Oh, it's no problem." She hefted the large bag at her feet. "I've got my valise right here."

"I'll take you, Miss Delilah," Logan offered gallantly.

"This is all I brought, gentlemen. If you'll just show me the way. . ."

"Well, you beat me!" Alisa exclaimed.

"Not me," Miriam confessed. "I'm afraid I brought along half of the islands with me!"

While the women took her to the house, Paul pondered what he already knew about their pretty guest.

"From the letters I managed to receive. . .I'll bed down in the barn. . . . I've done it before. . . . This is all I brought. . . . " Her father was a gambler. The poor thing must have been dragged all over creation. What kind of man moved his daughter from place to place, not providing a decent roof over her head and making it so almost everything she owned could fit into one bag?

two

Delilah woke up the next morning and stretched groggily. As her eyes grew accustomed to the darkness, she tried to pick out a few details to remind her of where she was. It definitely didn't look like a barn or stable, nor did it seem like a hotel. The room contained only one window covered by a flap of fabric. The sun wasn't completely up yet, so everything stayed cast in varying degrees of shadow. She lay ensconced in a snug bed and could make out a chair against the wall. A small potbelly stove graced one corner, with a washstand taking up residence as the only other furniture in the room. She remembered placing her drawing supplies in the washstand's convenient drawer and filling only a few of the many pegs on the walls with her clothes. Long ago, she'd learned unpacking was the only way to make a strange room more comfortable.

The door opened quietly, bringing in a blast of frigid morning air. Miriam poked her head in the room to whisper, "Delilah?"

Yes, she remembered clearly now. She'd buried Papa and gone to Miriam's ranch, taking the home of one of the Chance brothers. She swung her legs over the side of the bed.

"I'm awake." Leaving the snug warmth of the bed, Delilah padded across the cool floor in her bare feet.

"I need to make breakfast, so I thought you'd like to watch before you have your first real lesson later today," Miriam invited.

Delilah nodded. "I'll be dressed in a minute." Miriam carefully closed the door, and Delilah crept over to the table where her valise sat. She changed out of her nightgown into her yellow cambric day dress. The dress she'd worn while traveling here currently boasted more dust than cloth, and she only owned one other. The primrose satin evening gown her father had purchased in a spurt of indulgence after a good gaming streak wasn't appropriate for ranch work. She'd brushed and braided her hair before bed last night, after Polly and Ginny Mae let her do the same for them. She quickly twisted the braid on top of her head and pinned it into place. She left the cabin as Alisa walked across the yard toward her.

"Good morning, Alisa."

"Good morning, Delilah. Did you sleep well?"

Delilah took enough time to assure the kindhearted woman that she had slept very well before hurrying into the main cabin.

"What are you going to make?" Delilah wanted to know what she was getting herself into.

"The men can hardly crack their eyes open without their morning coffee. Then I thought we'd start with something easy—scrambled eggs and diced ham." Miriam handed her the coffeepot. "If you'd like, you can pump this full of water."

Delilah did as she asked, then pulled out plates, glasses, knives, and forks to set the table.

Miriam brought out a salted ham hock. "Why don't you watch as I cut the first bit? Then you can try your hand at it." This seemed easy enough—Delilah didn't lack competence with a knife.

"All right, you try it." Miriam nodded her approval as Delilah started shaving and chopping. "You have a sharp eye and a steady hand. That's good." Together they finished the ham, and Delilah, starting to feel more comfortable, waited for further instructions. Miriam brought out a huge bowl.

"I still have plenty of eggs left from yesterday, so we're all set. You tap 'em on the edge of the bowl, like this." She demonstrated in one swift movement. "Then part the halves and let the egg run into the bowl. See?"

Miriam made it look absolutely effortless. Heartened, Delilah resolutely picked up an egg and brought it down on the rim of the bowl. With a crack that all but echoed in the morning stillness, the shell split completely and yellow goop slimed the tabletop.

Miriam started laughing. "Gently!" She wiped up the table with a rag and handed Delilah another egg. "All right, give it another shot."

Delilah put down the egg. "I don't want to waste them."

Miriam smiled. "That was just your first try. I did the very same thing. Try again."

This time, Delilah tapped it so gently, the shell didn't boast so much as a crack. She looked helplessly at Miriam.

"Just keep tapping it a little harder each time until you get the feel for it. Be careful, and you'll get it right." In no time at all, Delilah got the hang of it, and three dozen eggs floated in the bowl.

"Now what?"

"We stir it until the clear and the yellow run together. Here." She gave Delilah a wooden spoon, and Delilah followed her instructions, then poured half of the mixture into a large, greased skillet waiting on the stove.

"Mix it periodically and add in the ham." Miriam demonstrated. It cooked until a mess of scrambled eggs and ham sat ready to be put on a platter.

"Now try cooking the other half while I warm some bread."

Miriam pulled two loaves from the breadbox and began slicing.

Delilah took the pan and poured the rest of the eggs into it. She watched intently for it to bubble, then pounced to stir it as soon as it began. Some of the goop seemed stuck on the bottom.

"Miriam? Why do mine stick to the pan when yours didn't?"

Her cousin hustled over to take a look. "I forgot to tell you that you need to regrease the pan. It'll be difficult to scrub clean, but your eggs'll be fine. Just keep moving them around until they look like mine."

Pretty soon, they looked finished, and Delilah emptied the contents of the pan onto the platter. Following more advice, she filled the dirty pan with water from the pump.

Miriam had just finished placing butter and preserves on the table when Gideon wandered in. "Sure smells good in here, sweetheart."

"Thank you. Fresh coffee's on the stove, and Delilah here helped me make ham 'n' eggs for breakfast."

Gideon turned to Delilah. "Good morning, Delilah. If you're half the cook my Miriam is, we'll keep you busy for sure."

Delilah confessed. "Actually, this is the first time I've cooked anything. I hope it tastes all right."

Logan and Bryce stumbled into the room toward the basin, followed by Dan and Paul. Dan started cutting toast into little strips and putting them on a tiny plate. Paul grabbed the milk and filled two small glasses. He turned to her.

"Miss Delilah, would you like milk, water, or coffee this morning?" His gaze was as penetrating as the day before, and her nerves tingled as heat spread through her.

"I'd like the milk, please." She loved fresh milk. "And please just call me Delilah. No 'miss' is needed." That was for sure.

With her twenty-first birthday fast approaching, she knew most girls her age had already started families. Somehow, she didn't want this intriguing man to think of that every time they spoke.

"Delilah." He said it softly, testing it out, but the way he said it made it sound beautiful.

Titus came in, leading Alisa and their nieces. Everyone took a seat. Gideon presided at the head of the table, with Miriam on his right. Delilah hastened to sit on her other side. Dan sat to his left with Ginny Mae on his lap and Polly beside him, flanked by Alisa and Titus. Paul sat next to Delilah, with Logan beside him and Bryce at the end of the table. Delilah tried to ignore how they were packed so close, she could feel Paul's warmth.

After everyone settled in, Delilah jumped a bit when Paul clasped her hand in his until she realized they had all joined hands for prayer. She only wished she could be a part of something so special.

For now, she'd just pretend that she wasn't someone they'd taken in out of charity. She listened as Gideon spoke of his appreciation for all of their blessings and asked God to be with them during the day to come. It seemed strange that they'd think God, who was so big and busy, would be right beside each of them all day long. Perhaps it just feels that way because they have each other to care about.

Paul's hand swallowed hers. It almost made her feel dainty and feminine sitting next to him with her hand cocooned in his warm, work-roughened palm. She stifled a pang of regret when the prayer ended, and after a slight reassuring squeeze, he let go. She sat as an outsider once again amid morning chatter as everyone passed around platters of eggs and bread with the coffee.

❧

I don't want to let go, Paul realized. He didn't even know why he'd sat next to her. Usually he took the place at the end of the table where Bryce sat today. Logan sent him a peeved look, but Paul watched Delilah hop like a frightened rabbit to be next to Miriam, and before he knew it, he squeezed beside her at the table. He'd felt her quick intake of breath when he'd first grasped her palm. Now he didn't want to let go of the warm, soft, slender hand nestled so sweetly in his.

She towered over Miriam on the other side of her, but the crown of her head came about equal to his nose. She reminded him of that old fairy tale Alisa told the girls. The one about the girl who walked into the bears' house and tested everything out. Delilah felt not too big, not too small, but just right. She smelled so feminine and delicate, but he didn't feel like he crushed her hand, either, which brought him back to the odd little war going on inside of him.

Paul knew the prayer would end any minute, but he just hadn't quite convinced himself to let go. Her dress—the color of marigolds—made her look like a ray of sunshine, and he wanted to enjoy her warmth a little longer. When everyone said, "Amen," he compromised and gave her hand a slight squeeze before withdrawing.

"Your breakfasts make it worth gettin' up, Miriam." Bryce's praise was well earned.

"Thank you, Bryce, but I think Delilah deserves most of the credit this morning. It's the first time she's ever cooked." Miriam's response had everyone peering at their new houseguest.

"You did a fine job, a mighty fine job." Logan shoveled eggs with gusto as everyone congratulated Delilah.

Even Polly chimed in. "Yeah. I haven't ate crunchy eggs

since Aunt Miri-Em came."

Silence fell as the menfolk became intently interested in their coffee and Delilah blushed. "I must've gotten some shell into the bowl. I'm so sorry."

"It's all right," Alisa assured her as she inspected Polly's plate. "A little bit never hurt anyone, I'm sure."

"What are you doing, Auntie Alisa? I like my crunchy eggs!" Polly snatched back her plate. Paul couldn't help it; he started to chuckle. Soon everyone joined in, even Dan.

"Crunchy eggs!" Dan grinned at his little daughter. "Well, Princess Polly, if you like your crunchy eggs, you can go ahead and eat them. Won't do you any harm."

After the laughter stopped, Paul faced Delilah. Her cheeks flushed. "Maybe little Polly got a bit of shell in hers, but I've never tasted better eggs 'n' ham." He couldn't remember the last time he'd enjoyed breakfast so much.

❧

After breakfast, the men went out to their usual duties while the women cleaned up. It took Delilah half of eternity to scrub the skillet clean, but finally she finished.

"Delilah," Miriam offered, "since you arrived yesterday evening, you didn't have much of an opportunity to wash up after traveling. I'll bet your hands are pretty well soaked after that pan, but if you'd like, we can fill the tub so you can have a bath. After you're done, we'll dunk the girls."

"That would be wonderful, Miriam. I'll start pumping the water." While Miriam dandled Ginny Mae on her lap and worked with Polly on colors and numbers, Alisa and Delilah heated pots of water and hefted them to the old washtub they'd hauled in from the barn. When they'd set everything up, Delilah hurried to fetch her soap.

Once behind the screen, she got out of her clothing as

quickly as possible and slid into the bath. She supposed the tub was barely big enough for the largest of the brothers to hunch into, but it gave her enough room to lean back as long as she bent her legs. Mindful that the little ones would be next, she picked up the soap instead of soaking. It wouldn't be fair to leave them with a cold bath after she luxuriated in the relaxing warmth. After she filled her hair with suds, she reached for the basin of fresh water next to her. When she'd scrubbed out all the dirt and achiness, she reluctantly climbed from the tub to help Miriam and Alisa with the girls.

When she came out from behind the partition, Miriam looked at her in surprise. "That was awfully fast."

"Usually we enjoy a soak for as long as we can. It's one of the comforts around here." Alisa spoke as she helped Polly undress.

"I enjoyed every minute," Delilah praised. "I just didn't want the water to be cold for the girls. I feel so much more like myself now that I'm clean again."

"Why don't you try to dry your hair and braid it while we take care of the children?"

Delilah gratefully took Miriam's advice and toweled her hair a bit more, only to realize she'd forgotten her brush. She excused herself and went out once more. The sun glowed cheerfully in the blue sky, so full of life she slowed her pace to enjoy the beauty of the day. Rather than braid her hair alone in the small cabin, she picked up her brush and trekked back to the kitchen. After living without the company of women for so long, she found herself eager to spend time with Miriam and Alisa. *I might as well enjoy it while it lasts.*

&

Paul shaded his eyes and scanned the sky. It could only be about ten o'clock, but for some reason, he hankered for lunchtime. At any rate, he needed to head back for some more tacks. The stretch of fence they'd been fixing needed more help than they'd thought, considering they'd worked on it a few weeks before.

He strode over to where Speck, his brown-and-white paint, calmly grazed. He swung into the saddle and trotted over to Titus. "I'm heading back for some more tacks." At his brother's nod, he turned Speck toward the barn and cantered off. As the house came into sight, he spotted a flash of yellow as Delilah came out of the kitchen. He watched as she slowed her pace, enjoying the sun. Her head tilted back for a moment, and black waves tumbled over her shoulders. His throat went dry.

As she disappeared into the room he'd given up for her, he spurred Speck over to the barn before hitching the horse. *I'm parched*, he told himself as he headed toward the kitchen for a cup. Yep. Being so close, it made sense to go get a cool drink from the pump rather than slug some of the tepid water from his canteen. That was all there was to it. Who could blame him if he stayed a couple of moments to tickle the girls? Good uncles needed to spend time with their nieces, and since the women had arrived, he missed having a day a week with the girls. If Delilah happened to come back into the kitchen while he was there, it'd do no harm to see how she was getting along. He lengthened his stride toward the door.

"Hello, Paul." Alisa didn't hide her surprise at seeing him. From the damp towel on the floor by his barefooted niece, he reckoned she'd hauled Ginny Mae from the tub and was just buttoning up the last button. When she made as if to hand the toddler off to Miriam, he quickly intercepted.

Delilah glided into the room like a beam of sunlight carrying a brush. She stopped cold at the sight of him.

"Don't mind me. I came by for some tacks and thought I'd grab a drink before I got back out there." He ignored the knowing glance Miriam sent him and forgave her amusement when she jumped in.

"That's right, and he's lending a hand with Ginny Mae here for a moment until you're finished fixing your hair. Take a seat by the fire so your hair will dry a bit faster."

Delilah nodded and took a seat. Paul busied himself by drying Ginny Mae's hair, but he watched Delilah gently guide the brush stroke after stroke through her magnificent mane. When she started braiding, nimble fingers slipping through and weaving those black tresses, he became transfixed. The agility with which she performed the ritual showed it was a common one, but it seemed intimate since it was something usually done in private. By the time she'd finished putting her hair up, he wanted nothing more than to pull the pins out and run his fingers through it, testing its weight and silky texture.

She went out to the pump and filled a glass with water. As soon as she'd finished, she walked around the table. His breath caught as she stooped beside him and gently took Ginny Mae from his arms, giving him the cool water. She smelled wonderful—like fresh snow and violets.

As he walked back to the barn, he decided that lunchtime couldn't come soon enough.

three

After breakfast the next morning, Delilah followed Miriam into the barn with trepidation. She'd meant it when she said she wanted to learn everything about running the household, but somehow she'd never figured milking cows fit into it. She'd rather be in the vegetable garden with Alisa. Now she'd just have to make the best of it. *I like milk, so that's something, at least.*

The two creatures shared a large stall. Delilah watched as Miriam set a stool beside one of the beasts, then sat down and motioned for Delilah to come closer. Determinedly, Delilah strode over.

"Ready? First, take hold of one of Mister's teats, and—"

"Mister?" Delilah cut Miriam off. Even she knew this cow couldn't possibly be a male.

Miriam grinned. "Polly named them. This one's 'Mister' and the other's 'Sir.' Since she practiced her manners so well, the guys just didn't have the heart to tell her no."

It made perfect sense, so Delilah only giggled for a couple of minutes. Then they shifted their attention back to the lesson at hand.

"After you grab a pair, you tug and squeeze. Like this." A stream of white milk ran into the bucket. "Want to try?"

Not really. Delilah eyed Mister doubtfully but nodded anyway. Miriam got off the tiny stool so Delilah could perch on it. At least the cow wasn't moving. She hesitantly reached for the udder.

"That's it. Now tug downward and squeeze." Delilah did, and a squirt of milk splashed off the side of the bucket.

"Try to aim it into the bucket."

Well, why didn't she say so? Aiming posed no problem. Delilah compensated and caught the hang of milking in no time. While Delilah finished Mister, Miriam milked Sir, and before long, they completed the task.

"We'll make fresh butter today," Miriam decided as they carried their milk pails to the kitchen. They'd just set the buckets on the table when they heard voices outside.

⁊

They'd finished driving the herd to the next grazing pasture and were moving the bulls when a raven caught Paul's eye. Its wings shone the same smoky black as Delilah's hair. Unfortunately, an ornery bull chose that moment to break free and charge straight for him. After years of tending a ranch, Paul handled this sort of thing often enough, but for once it caught him off guard. He spurred Speck to zig when he should have zagged, and by the time he realized his mistake, he lay on the ground with a sharp pain throbbing up his arm.

Logan and Dan took charge of the bull, and Bryce reached Paul first, only to immediately check on how Speck fared.

"Anything other than a few bumps and bruises?" Gideon's concerned tone brought little comfort as Paul nodded.

"My arm." He gritted his teeth and awaited the pronouncement as Gideon prodded.

"Probably broken. We'll have to take you back to Miriam so she can have a look." Gideon hefted him up. It took both Bryce and Gideon to help get Paul into Splotch's saddle; then Gideon gave him a wary look. "You okay to ride?"

"Yeah."

"You lie just as lousy as you look." Gideon swung up behind

him. Bryce followed with Speck as they rode back to the house.

After the men had gotten off the horse by the house, Miriam and Delilah dashed out to see what had happened. Paul left the explanations to Gideon.

"Speck lost him when they dodged an angry bull. I think he's broken his arm."

"Take him on into the kitchen." Everyone trooped behind, and Paul felt like a first-rate numbskull. How on earth would he prove himself a good protector and provider if he couldn't manage to stay on a horse? He'd decided after supper last night that Delilah was the woman for him. Maybe it seemed like a quick decision, but Papa had been the same way with Mama, and besides, there were dozens of men to every one woman out here. He needed to act fast. Of course, he'd be going slower now if he'd managed to break his arm. His forearm had already puffed up. Yep, that was attractive, all right.

He took a seat and grimaced as Miriam gently turned his arm. "Can you wiggle your fingers?" He complied, then sucked in a quick breath at the fresh flash of pain. Stupid thing hurt like anything, but the last thing he was gonna do with Delilah standing right beside him was holler about it. He snuck a peek at her face and gained some satisfaction at the expression of compassion on her delicate features.

"I broke my wrist years ago." She reached out and clasped his good hand. Warmth shot through him, but this time, he enjoyed the tingling sensation.

While he'd been distracted, someone brought in some straight pieces of wood and bandages. Miriam confirmed Gideon's assessment.

"You've broken your arm, but it seems like a clean break near the wrist. I'll have to splint it and put you in a sling,

Paul. You won't be able to ride for at least a couple of weeks. For today, I think you should take some of this." She plunked a glass of water on the table in front of him. From the way Miriam said it, he knew she'd laced it with laudanum. He shook his head.

"I'm not taking that." Since Delilah had begun holding his hand, the pain had stopped being so sharp.

Miriam retreated. "Paul, we all know you're a strong man who gives as good as he gets." That sounded better. He nodded his agreement.

She continued. "Do you remember the first night I came here?" Uh-oh. She'd tricked him. He scowled at her.

"You gave me laudanum after Logan brained me, right?"

He had no choice but to admit it. "What of it?" Now he sounded surly—typically more Dan's territory than his.

"So if you can give as good as you get, you should be able to take what you give to others." The pronouncement held no logical flaws, but he gave one last argument.

"I'll be fine—just fine—without it." He felt Delilah squeeze his hand and he turned to her.

"Wise men can admit when they need a little help. There's no shame in that, but there is some in causing yourself more pain than necessary." From her serious tone, he realized she spoke from watching her father's addiction to gambling ruin his life. It also crossed his mind that being stuck around the homestead wouldn't be such a bad thing for the next month or so. Staying close to the house meant sticking close to her—but only if he wasn't asleep the whole time. This called for a compromise.

"I'll be sure and take it before bed to make sure I sleep but not now. If your argument holds, Miriam, that's fair since I only gave you laudanum at night."

Miriam gave in graciously. "I'll hold you to that, Paul."

&

After trussing Paul up like a turkey—his words, not hers—Miriam sent the rest of the men back out to the grazing fields and handed Paul a bucket of slop for the pigs.

"This morning I intended to teach Delilah how to take care of the yard livestock. We'd just finished milking Mister and Sir when you rode up. Alisa's watching the girls, and I need to start on lunch. I hadn't gathered the eggs this morning so I could show Delilah. It still needs to be done. The chickens need to be fed, and the pigs slopped, too. If you feel up to it, take Delilah with you and teach her. She's a quick learner." With that, Miriam shooed them both out of her kitchen.

Delilah found herself standing outside with Paul, trying to decide whether or not she felt happy with the situation. She'd learned long ago not to let herself be caught alone with a man—they couldn't be trusted. But here she stood. She couldn't do or say anything to get out of it without insulting Miriam or Paul. Not to mention that, of all the brothers, it had to be Paul—the one she was most drawn to and least comfortable around. Well, Dan probably made her more uncomfortable, but Miriam wouldn't push her into spending time with him.

Why couldn't it be Bryce, more concerned with his animals, or either Titus or Gideon, who couldn't keep their eyes off their wives? She'd even prefer Logan, who couldn't seem to stop himself from staring. Nope, she wasn't that lucky. Paul, the unexpectedly intriguing giant broke his arm. She'd even held his hand for some reason she couldn't recall. The man who gently held Ginny Mae and dried her duck fluff hair, whose touch sent tingles down Delilah's spine, would teach her to slop pigs.

A lot of thoughts raced through that pretty head. Paul wondered what those thoughts might be. He figured they had something to do with the fact Delilah wasn't comfortable being alone with him. As unencouraging as that might be, she'd held his hand earlier while Miriam looked at his arm, which meant that, even if chances were slim, they existed. He should say something to set her at ease.

"Shall we go?" It wasn't exactly a proposal, but it was a start.

Delilah looked at the basket of chicken feed she held. "Do you want to feed the chickens first?"

"Sure. The henhouse is this way." They walked over to the coop. Actually, calling it a chicken cupboard would be more accurate since its two doors swung on hinges that opened outward. Bryce had invented it years ago. Given that all of the brothers were too big to squeeze into a small aisle in the middle of a crowded coop, he simply made a structure about six feet high with a single wall filled with rows of nesting boxes in the back. As usual, the doors stayed open so the flightless birds could peck around their fenced-in yard during the day.

"The eggs are in those boxes. You just have to stick your hand in and find them. First, we scatter the feed in the far corner of the yard, so the hens will be distracted. This is springtime, though, so a few of 'em are bound to be setting."

"Setting?"

"Yep. They just sit on their eggs day in and day out and don't want to move except to snatch some feed. If you run across one that comes back before the others or won't move, just let her be. It's actually best if you can sneak a few extra eggs into her nest, so she'll hatch them, too. In a little bit, she'll have a brood of baby chicks."

"All right, so first we scatter the feed. Over here?" She

started tossing handfuls in front of her.

"That's it. Now, when you've scattered some, be sure to scoot back—" His instructions came a bit too late, as the hungry cluck of chickens converged on the feed. . .and Delilah. She backed up against a fence. Paul waded through the squawking mass of feathers to help her edge away from the ravenous birds pecking very close to her feet.

"Thanks." The smile she shot him singed his heart like a lightning bolt. "They'd managed to corner me."

"You just didn't count on them being such greedy birds. The second the feed hits the ground, they're on their way. Now that they're good and distracted, we'll fill the basket with eggs."

He understood distraction all too well. She wore the same dress as yesterday, but the golden fabric hinted at the worth of its wearer.

They stepped into the coop and started rooting around for the eggs. "It's more like hunting eggs than gathering them, isn't it?" Delilah asked. "They hide them pretty well under all that straw and such."

"True. It's always like that when they're nesting. Sometimes a really determined hen will go into the taller weeds and build a secret nest for her eggs."

"I understand that. It's natural to want to protect what's yours, and who doesn't want to have some small space just to call their own?"

He'd like to call her his own, and he knew of a cozy little cabin they could share.

As the basket filled, one or two of the hens came back to settle on their nests again. He took some of the eggs and tucked them under the birds; then he led Delilah away from the coop. They dropped off the eggs in the kitchen, where

Miriam was checking on a roast. Paul picked up the slop bucket with his good hand, and they headed off again. It wasn't until he reached the hog pen that he realized they had a slight problem.

"Usually I just grab the handle with one hand, and the back of the bucket with the other, and pour it into the trough. . . ."

She understood the problem. "Need a hand?"

"Literally." He smiled.

"Here, I'm the one who's supposed to be learning, anyway."

He looked at her, then the bucket. "It's kind of heavy."

His angel squared her shoulders and gave him a determined look. "I carried buckets of milk this morning. Besides, if Miriam can do it, so can I."

So she had an independent streak. Good. He didn't want some gingerbread miss who'd crumble at a word. He handed her the bucket and watched as she dumped its contents over the side of the pen into the wooden trough.

Accustomed to dining at an earlier hour, the pigs were hungrier than usual. They snuffled over to plunge their snouts into the mess of grub. Delilah watched them thoughtfully.

"You know, they're kind of cute. Almost reminds me of. . ." Her voice trailed off, and he thought he knew why.

"Yep. They get almost as much food on themselves as in their mouths—just like Ginny Mae." That brought on another smile.

"I thought so, too, but I didn't want to compare such a precious little girl to a bunch of pigs."

"Well, since we both thought the same thing, there must be truth in it," he pointed out. "There's no harm in plain speaking."

"True, but honesty isn't a very common quality, is it?" She stated the observation with such quiet certainty, he wasn't sure how to respond.

"Why do you say that?" Though he wanted to know, he also aimed to fill the awkward silence as they walked back to the house.

"I'm not saying there aren't good people out there." Her eyes filled with resignation and regret. "You and your brothers seem to be some of them. But on the whole, people lie, or cheat, or hide things from others. Everyone makes decisions based on their own needs. That's the way of the world."

Paul knew she'd hopped from town to town with her father, that she didn't own much and wasn't married because of it. He hadn't thought of the people she'd been exposed to along the way—probably all drunks, hustlers, gamblers, and crooks. Little wonder she didn't have much faith in the general honesty of mankind.

"Everyone makes mistakes. It's a matter of how we deal with them before God. 'If we confess our sins, He is faithful and just to forgive us our sins, and to cleanse us from all unrighteousness.' "

"If He's able to do that, then why doesn't He help the people who can't help themselves but want to?" Her wistful tone hinted that she thought of her father's addiction to the gaming tables, but her statement chilled Paul to the core. Could it be that the woman he wanted to make his wife didn't even trust the Lord?

Dear Lord, am I wrong in thinking this is the woman Thou hast made to be my helpmate? She's been hurt in so many ways, but I see Thy grace in her smile. Please give me the words to soothe her and bring her closer to Thee.

"He works in mysterious ways, Delilah, so we don't always know when He's working in us. That doesn't mean He's not with us, but it doesn't mean He necessarily makes things the way we want them."

She refused to meet his gaze any longer. "Then what's the point of believing in Him?" she whispered sadly before turning and walking away.

four

Two mornings later, Delilah eyed her primrose evening dress with distaste. Today was laundry day, so at least she'd get her traveling frock clean, but she'd been wearing the yellow one for three days straight. Unfortunately, she couldn't very well don the primrose satin evening gown to do laundry. That meant the yellow wouldn't get washed.

Well, one clean dress was better than none, and she'd take what she could get. As she prepared to get dressed, she heard a knock on the door.

"Who is it?" She tried to make her voice loud enough for the person to hear, but soft enough so that it wouldn't wake Bryce and Logan in the next cabin.

"Alisa. May I come in?"

Delilah hurriedly put on her robe before unlatching the door.

Alisa walked in. "You know it's wash day today, right? Well, I know the dress you wore when you arrived was done in from traveling, and you've been wearing the yellow one all week. I've got plenty of dresses, so I thought this might fit." She held out a deep green day dress.

Despite knowing from Miriam that Alisa had recently inherited her wealth and that Alisa probably did own plenty of dresses, her kind gesture touched Delilah. "Thank you, but I really couldn't. You've already done so much for me."

"This shade looks awful on me, but with your coloring, it'll look fabulous on you. I only brought it back because I thought we could make something from the fabric—it's a bit long. Luckily, you're taller than I am. Why don't you try it on while I go set the table?" With that, Alisa placed the dress on Delilah's just-made bed and whisked out of the room.

It would be rude to refuse the beautiful garment. Delilah pulled it on, relieved to notice the small pockets concealed in the skirt. The sleeves and hemline both fell a bit short, but otherwise it fit perfectly. She always rolled up her sleeves, anyway, so that hardly mattered, and hopefully she could let down the hem. For now, it was passable. She put up her hair and hurried to the kitchen to see if she could help with breakfast. Thanks to Miriam, she knew how to make eggs 'n' ham, stew, biscuits, cobbler, coffee, bread, bacon, and oatmeal. Well, she didn't remember how much flour and so forth by heart just yet, but she could follow the instructions well enough. Today she'd learn how to prepare flapjacks.

When she entered the kitchen, Alisa smiled. "See, it would be positively criminal for you not to wear that shade. Other than it being a little short, it's perfect for her, isn't it, Miriam?"

"She's right. Somehow the forest green suits your dark hair and light eyes. It's very becoming. I've already put on the coffee and made the flapjack batter. Are you ready to cook them?"

Delilah stifled a pang of disappointment over missing how to make the batter. She enjoyed cooking, even though she'd made a few minor mistakes—like with the eggs. Soon enough, she started ladling batter onto a large skillet, pouring smooth circles. Watching vigilantly for the circles to start bubbling, she lifted the edge of the flapjacks to make sure they'd cooked enough before flipping them.

Even though she tried to be careful, one slid off the griddle onto the stove, and somehow one ended up on the floor before she really got the hang of it. Miriam and Alisa laughed with her when she made a mistake and helped her make what had to be more than two dozen good-sized pancakes.

By the time the men wandered in, everything was ready. They all took their places, and this time, Paul said grace. Delilah sat at his injured left side, so she rested her hand on his shoulder. She might not believe all of what they said during prayer time or even at nighttime Bible readings, but she relished the feeling of closeness and the warmth of family.

"Dear heavenly Father, although we cannot see Thee, we know Thou art always with us. . . ."

How can we know He is always with us if we can't see Him?

"Please guide us through this day and bless the food Thou hast placed at our table. . . ."

Humph. Paul must mean the food Miriam, Alisa, and I placed at the table.

"Let us feel Thy presence and remember to thank Thee for the blessings Thou hast given us. . . ."

Well, she didn't know about feeling God's presence, but she did feel blessed to be with Miriam and Alisa and Polly and Ginny. . .even Paul. She hadn't made up her mind about the rest yet.

"And a special thanks to Thee for bringing Miriam's cousin here. We're glad to have her with us. . . ."

Miriam's cousin? His words warmed her heart until she really thought about it. Paul thought God brought her to Chance Ranch? Wouldn't that mean He'd let her father die? How could that be right?

Maybe it was a kind thing to let him go, a tiny voice inside her spoke up. You know how much unhappiness he felt that he never lived up to his promises to you. Traveling all the time and the pressure of not winning were slowly killing him, anyway. Papa loved you. He'd be relieved to know you ended up here safe and sound.

Delilah tried to choke back her tears. She couldn't think about that now. After taking a deep breath, she realized the prayer was over. Belatedly, she removed her hand from Paul's shoulder. To give herself something to do, she picked up the syrup jug and started passing it around.

"Are you all right?" Paul's quiet question unnerved her even more. When she faced him, she needed to take a deep breath.

"I'll be fine. I'm just. . ." She paused. "Why don't you let me cut up those pancakes for you? You'll have to tell me if they're any good. Miriam made the batter, but if they're burned, it's my fault." She busied herself with her fork and knife.

"All right." Again, he spoke softly so the others wouldn't easily overhear. "I won't push you, but we'll talk sooner or later."

She didn't want to think about what that meant and strengthened her resolve not to get too close to this man. He understood her far better than he had any right to, and it flustered her.

"Alisa, Delilah, and I would like to go to town tomorrow." Miriam's voice thankfully pulled her attention away. "Paul should go with us so Doc Morris can have a peek at his arm."

For some reason, Gideon didn't look too happy. "Normally, that'd be fine, but since Paul only has one good arm, I'd prefer you wait until one of the rest of us can go with you."

Everyone listened in, and Titus, Bryce, Logan, and even Dan nodded their agreement.

Miriam stood her ground. "Without Paul, you already have fewer hands to take care of the ranch, and we need to get some supplies."

"I'm sorry, sweetheart. I don't want the three of you women going to town alone. It's not safe."

Alisa chimed in. "We're just going to the Whites' general store. With Paul along, we ought to be fine. Even with only one sound arm, he's still stronger than any two of the town boys."

"I agree with Gideon." Titus threw in his two cents' worth. "You'll have to wait a bit."

"Besides, you know it isn't often we get to go to town." The hangdog look on Logan's face made Delilah smile, it was so comical. Bryce focused on his plate.

Paul studied the women. "What is it you need?"

Miriam seemed to welcome his practical question. "We're low on sugar and could use some baking soda and flour, too. I wanted to teach Delilah how to make baked apples, but we don't have enough. I need some oil for cooking and a new scrub brush, and I'd like to pick up a few things for the baby before I can't make it to town anymore."

"I love baked apples." Bryce's hopeful comment earned him black looks from his brothers.

"I don't take any offense at what Gideon said," Paul stated. "It's a matter of protection."

"What if I proved that we could protect ourselves?" Guffaws met Delilah's question.

"Well, if you can prove that, missy, you can go wherever you want." Dan obviously thought she couldn't, or he wouldn't have made the promise.

"Do you all mean that?" In her experience, men thought women were helpless. That made dirty, paunchy, foul-breathed drunks dangerous—which is precisely why she'd learned how to protect herself at an early age. Now as the strapping Chance men winked slyly at each other and gave hearty, "Oh, sure's," that assumption finally worked in her favor.

"All right, then. As soon as you're all done with your flapjacks, we'll go outside," Delilah decided.

Miriam tugged on her too-short sleeve. "Do you know what you're doing, Delilah?"

That tiny whisper reminded Delilah of how different they really were. "Trust me, Miriam. I have a few tricks of my own."

Dan threw his napkin on the table. "I'm ready. I can't wait to see this. I'm going to go put Polly and Ginny Mae in the play yard."

"If you're ready, I'd suggest you all get your pistols and meet me on the south side of the barn." The men stared at her.

"What for?"

"You'll see soon enough. Miriam, Alisa, would you join me, please?"

◦❧◦

After the three women exited the room, Paul looked at his brothers. The expressions ranged from surprised to confused. Dan clearly expected to be entertained, but Paul held a few suspicions. Competency with a firearm became a necessity on the frontier—even for women—but marksmanship denoted long practice of the skill.

He stood up and strode to the door. Logan, Bryce, Titus, and Gideon quickly followed. Dan stayed to the back, with a girl tucked under each arm. When they got to the barn, Delilah quickly outlined the plan.

First, the girls would watch from a safe distance, tucked into a large shipping crate pushed against the barn. Then everyone participating in the makeshift "contest" would take turns shooting at a large knothole in a slab of wood Bryce leaned against the fence. They all inspected the target up close. Gideon cleared his throat. "Couple of close shots, and that board is going to be nothing but toothpicks."

"We'll use a bale of hay." Dan hiked toward the barn door and called over his shoulder, "Just stick a paper on it and stab a hole as the bull's-eye."

Soon, a pencil dot marked the center of the knothole.

"There won't be a bull's-eye left after seven holes are put in it," Logan protested.

"Six," Dan smirked.

"We'll be able to declare a winner, at any rate," Bryce decided.

"How many paces?" Titus asked.

"I'd think ten would be enough, since the test is about self-defense. Agreed?"

Paul figured she was a fair shot, but so were all the Chance men. He resolved not to let her win, no matter how disappointed she'd look later. It wasn't good for a woman to get the idea she could go scampering off wherever and whenever she liked. He'd rather beat her this once than have her run into trouble later.

"Who goes first?" Miriam asked.

"You'll go from youngest to oldest," Alisa directed.

"What about ladies first?" Paul broke in. It would be nice to gauge the competition.

"I'd prefer to go last." Delilah ruled that out. "Logan, you're up."

Logan measured off ten paces, turned, and aimed. A few heartbeats after he fired, everyone rushed to the paper to see how he'd fared. Alisa whipped out her measuring tape.

"Two and a quarter inches left of center," she proclaimed as Miriam made a tiny L by the hole.

"Stupid thing always did shoot a bit to the left," Logan muttered about his Navy Colt. Bryce took the next turn. His bullet hit too far right but did slightly better.

"One and seven-eighths inches from center," Alisa measured, and Miriam scribbled a minuscule B.

Titus managed to shoot a bit high. "Best yet, darling," a not-quite impartial Alisa congratulated. "One and a quarter inch from center."

"I object," Logan broke in. "Titus sweet-talked the judge!" Miriam assured him Alisa measured correctly, and the competition continued. Paul's turn came quickly.

Now he'd take his chance to prove that, even if he'd gotten thrown from his horse, he could still hold his own. He issued a swift prayer. *Lord, I know pride goes before a fall, but since I already fell this week, I'd be mighty obliged if You'd consider it even and let me do well today.*

He counted off ten long paces and aimed. While Alisa and Miriam hustled over to the target, he held his breath.

The call of "a half inch right from center" was music to his ears. Anyone would be hard pressed to beat that—even Gideon, who Paul viewed as his only real competition. He risked a look at Delilah. Her appreciative smile took him by surprise, because she seemed completely unruffled. Could she possibly beat him?

Dan shot a little low, "one inch from center," and Gideon matched Paul's shot with "a half inch left from center." The only way Delilah could possibly win would be to shoot dead center between the holes Paul's and Gideon's bullets made.

"Would you like to borrow my gun?" Gideon offered.

To the astonishment of everyone present, Delilah pulled a small Derringer from a pocket in her dress.

"I always carry one of my own." The brothers watched, flabbergasted, as she took ten strides, hardly bothered to aim, and fired.

Paul prayed fervently as Alisa measured. "A quarter inch from center, low." Delilah had won.

❧

She couldn't remember the last time she'd had so much fun, Delilah decided. Logan seemed awed, Bryce eyed her with a new respect, Dan looked downright mutinous, while Gideon and Titus moped. As for Paul, she averted her face from his piercing gaze.

"I suppose that means we get to go to town, after all, ladies," she said, addressing a beaming Alisa and grinning Miriam.

"I don't think so," Dan growled. "You needed to prove that you three women would be protected. What happens after your one shot?" To underscore his point, he snatched the compact gun from her grasp.

"It won't do you much good, and I don't like the thought of you carrying this around my daughters." He stalked off.

Quick as a flash, Delilah grabbed the small knife she kept strapped to her ankle. "Daniel Chance, you will return that." Her voice held a warning even he couldn't completely ignore.

He stopped and turned around. "I don't think so." The next minute, Daniel groped the top of his head and started looking around. Obviously, he didn't understand—no sudden breeze had snatched his hat.

His much-used hat hung pinned to the barn behind him by a small knife with a mother-of-pearl handle. As he gaped at it, Delilah swept past, pulled the knife from the wall in a single jerk, and turned to face Daniel, holding his hat behind her back.

"My gun, if you please." She held out a commanding hand.

Daniel all but gnashed his teeth before giving in and getting his hat in return.

A pleased smile spread across her face. "Thank you."

٭

"My hat. My poor hat." Dan sat on his bed, looking mournfully at the hat he held.

Paul bit back a grin. "You shouldn't have tried to take her gun, Dan."

"A girl like that has no business owning a gun. Or being able to handle a knife like that."

"Think about it, Daniel. Her father gambled his way from town to town, dragging her along with him. Who knows what kind of trouble a pretty woman like her ran into? I hate to think of it, but she probably did have occasion to use them." Paul saw the light dawn in Dan's eyes as his habitual scowl deepened.

"Well, she won't need 'em here, that's for sure. And neither will my girls. If anyone comes near a'one of them, I'll skin him alive. Her papa didn't do right by her, poor thing."

Dan's words just about summed up Paul's own feelings on the subject. Paul punched his pillow into shape with more force than was absolutely necessary.

Maybe her father didn't, but I will.

five

Long before the sun came up the next morning, Delilah awoke to someone knocking on her door. Apparently, the Chance clan didn't think she'd get up on her own, as this was the second time in as many days. Hastily pulling on her wrapper, she heard Miriam's urgent whisper.

"Delilah? Delilah!"

Delilah wrenched open the door, and Miriam, clad in only her nightgown and robe, scurried in.

"What's wrong?" Delilah demanded, dozens of scenarios in which one or more of this precious family were gravely injured.

"Nothing's wrong!" Upon closer scrutiny, Miriam's face, flushed with cold, seemed more excited than frantic.

"Do you remember how we made butter the day Paul broke his arm, since we could get store credit for it?"

Delilah nodded, confused. "Yes, but it's so early in the morning, Miriam! What's going on?"

"Well, Gideon said last night that any credit I managed to wrangle from Mr. White could be ours to spend however Alisa and I choose!"

"That's wonderful, but my mind's not working well enough this early to figure out why you're jumping like a grasshopper." Obviously, her cousin had lost her mind.

"I need your help, and the sooner we start, the better off we'll be. I don't want to go to Alisa and Titus's cabin, so it's up to us to fetch the cream from the springhouse and make as much butter as we can this morning!"

Suddenly, all became clear. Miriam wanted the extra currency for their trip to town. Even Delilah knew that pregnant women sometimes had odd starts, but apparently Miriam hadn't gone mad, after all.

"All right. Go get dressed, and I'll meet you in the barn so we can milk Sir and Mister."

"Thank you, Delilah!" Miriam rushed out of the room.

Delilah put on her freshly laundered blue serge traveling frock. The widest of her skirts, it permitted her to easily get in and out of the buckboard. Besides, they were setting out early, and the heavy fabric would afford more protection against the sharp morning air.

Throwing on a heavy shawl, she tromped out to the barn. Miriam was already there, starting on Sir. Delilah set a stool next to Mister and started milking. When they'd finished, they hauled the fresh milk to the springhouse.

They brought the cream back into the kitchen, where the paddle churn waited. Delilah scooped in some cream and started churning while Miriam scurried about, feeding the chickens and pigs and gathering eggs—until Alisa came into the kitchen.

"Is it time to start breakfast already?" Miriam couldn't disguise her disappointment. They usually began breakfast at about five o'clock. Since she and Delilah started working almost two hours before, they'd expected to get more done.

"No, I just woke up early and couldn't get back to sleep. It's about half past four now." Since Alisa had brought back a mantel clock from her old home, she alone knew exact time. "You wanted to get an early start on packing things for town, too?"

"Gideon said we could spend all the credit we get for eggs and butter on whatever we like!"

"Let's get going, then!" Apparently, Alisa was quicker on the uptake than Delilah early in the morning. "Where do we stand now?"

Delilah did some quick tabulating. "We made eight bricks on Thursday, and there are still nine in the springhouse from before that. I've finished one this morning, and this batch is ready for rinsing." Alisa took over the churn while Delilah rinsed and pressed the butter.

"Miriam, how are we for eggs?"

"The day Paul broke his arm, we didn't collect the eggs until after breakfast, which was about three dozen. Yesterday we had flapjacks, so I saved another dozen. This morning I collected another three, so we have seven dozen to take to town." Miriam finished packing the eggs and started to pick up a crate. In a few quick steps, Delilah took it from her.

"You shouldn't be lifting anything in your condition. If I catch you trying to haul anything today, I'm going to side with the men and say you shouldn't go to town." She made the warning as ominous as she could, but Miriam just shrugged and started the coffee before getting to work on the oatmeal. Delilah stacked the crates outside the door.

"Not bad." Alisa approved as she plopped the butter into the bowl for the next washing. "I'll have another load of butter done this morning. We should leave one in the springhouse since we'll be wanting to do some baking and one more for the oatmeal this morning. Delilah, how does that add up?"

"Nineteen for town." They didn't have much time left, so everyone buckled down. Delilah just started pressing the final brick of butter when the men began trickling in. First came Gideon, with a smile and a peck on the cheek for Miriam. Logan and Bryce came in next. Logan looked suspiciously at the pot on the stove.

"What's that?"

"Oatmeal," Delilah answered. Logan groaned and grumped about for the remainder of breakfast. Not only was he stuck at home while Paul and the women got to go to town, he couldn't look forward to the standard three feasts a day. Delilah thought the oatmeal deserved more credit. Miriam added generous amounts of sugar during the cooking, and the butter and preserves on the table let everybody doctor theirs as little or as much as they liked.

During breakfast, the women handed out last-minute instructions. Dan would watch Ginny Mae and Polly. Miriam set out bread and meat for them to make sandwiches for lunch. As soon as the meal ended, the men loaded half of the steer they'd butchered yesterday into the buckboard, along with the eggs Miriam packed while the women did the dishes.

Usually, one of the men would drive, but since Paul had a broken arm, the responsibility fell to the most competent woman. Alisa took the reins because Miriam's delicate condition excluded her from taking on any strenuous activities.

Paul insisted Miriam sit beside Alisa rather than ride in the back with half of a dead steer, which left Delilah to share the cramped space with him. She took care to sit on his right side so she wouldn't bump his injured arm. Still, it didn't do much good if he was as uncomfortable as she felt. Her arm pressed against his, and they hunched so close, even their legs touched. As usual, sitting next to him made her feel almost petite, but the crowded seating arrangement wasn't to her liking. Why did I ever put on this shawl? Delilah wondered. The morning was nothing if not overly warm.

☙

Usually Paul opted to ride Speck rather than pile into the

wagon, but for once, he didn't mind being packed in like a sardine. Despite the butchered steer sharing the space, he relished Delilah's company. Noticing how she took special care to sit on his right gave him an idea. He casually moved a crate of eggs between him and the side of the wagon, pretending to rest his arm on it. Hopefully, she'd never suspect he did it intentionally so they'd have less room.

It worked. The length of her leg pressed against his, her arm against his, and he could catch the scent of violets in her hair. He bit back a grin and leaned back to enjoy the next hour as they rode to town. Yep, he reckoned breaking his arm was probably the smartest thing he'd ever done.

They reached Reliable far too soon to his way of thinking. Miriam and Alisa hitched the horses while he jumped out of the wagon and swept Delilah down with his good arm. The men on the street jabbed each other and gawked at her. If he could, he'd have held on for a lot longer, but he needed to help Miriam. By the time they reached the back of the general store, a horde of bachelors straggled in behind them. Paul glared at each and every one of them, wishing he could make them all leave.

Reba White bustled out to the counter, beaming from ear to ear. "Miriam! Alisa! It's so good to see you again. How've y'all been?" She caught sight of Delilah. "And who's this pretty young thing?"

That let loose a torrent of remarks from the rabble behind them. "Yeah! Who's she?"

"Where'd she come from?"

"Marry me!"

"No, me!"

Paul stepped in front of the women and spoke in a low voice. His tone served as a warning. "This here is a guest at the Chance Ranch. If anybody wants to speak to the lady, they'll have to act like a gentleman. If you can't behave yourselves, you'll have more trouble than you can handle." Out of the corner of his eye, he saw that Delilah stood in front of Miriam, her hands in her pockets.

"Aw, you Chance boys have all the luck."

"It's not fair. There weren't no decent women in the town but Reba and Priscilla when Miriam came," another interrupted.

"And Gideon got her, and Titus snatched Alisa. You Chance men can't go 'round taking all the women to be found. Ain't neighborly."

General mutters of agreement rumbled as the throng moved closer. "Ya oughta introduce us proper-like."

Gus White came out from behind the curtain in the back of the store, brandishing a broom.

"Get out, you lazy good-fer-nothin's. You can't stick around hasslin' my customers."

"But Gus, we just wanna—Hey!"

Gus thwapped the dirty ruffian on the head with the broom. Paul didn't remember the last time he'd felt so much brotherly love for any soul as he bore Gus at that moment.

"I said git!" Gus punctuated his words with a well-placed prod to another man's backside as the crowd beat a hasty retreat.

"All right, all right. We're goin'. We didn't mean nothin'."

As soon as they left, Gus turned, his scowl replaced by a genial smile. "Hello, Mrs. Miriam, Mrs. Alisa. Ma'am. Howdy, Titus. What'dya do to your arm?"

"This un's Paul, Gus." Reba shook her head, then spoke to the women. "I declare, if there really were more women around here, he'd probably forget my name, too. Well, seems to me you've got some news to tell." She waited expectantly.

"Paul broke his arm, Reba, and this is my cousin, Delilah," Miriam quickly explained.

Reba gave Delilah an assessing once-over. "I'm right glad to see you, Miss Delilah. Don't worry none about that bunch—they're lonely, and you'll probably get more decent offers than indecent, if you take my meaning." She straightened her shoulders. "I'm afraid Doc Morris is out of town, Paul. Will you be all right?"

"Miriam already set the break, and it hasn't been troubling me too much. My arm'll be fine, Mrs. Reba. And how've you been?"

"Can't complain," Gus remarked. "What can we do for you folks today?"

Alisa rattled off a list of goods—rice, beans, flour, meal, sugar, spices, apples, cocoa, maple syrup, canning jars, buttons, and vegetable seeds—then turned to Paul. He added tacks, ammunition, spring tonic, and a salt lick to the list.

"We slaughtered a steer yesterday, Gus. It's out in the wagon." The Chance family never bothered with store credit if they could avoid it.

"Fair enough." Gus turned when he heard the door creak open. "I told everyone to get outta here."

"We heard." A wiry man made his way to the back of the store, followed by two others.

"Howdy, Paul," one of them greeted. "We done heard you broke your arm and figgered ya'd need a hand with unloadin' your wagon."

"Perfect." Gus ushered them back out the door and called to Paul, "That ought to be about even, after what you brought me last time," before turning back to the ladies.

❧

Delilah watched Paul leave with some regret. He'd been so strong when he stood up to that awful pack of men. True, they'd been more curious than dangerous, but there were some rough characters mingled in, and you never could tell when a crowd could turn into a mob. She knew how to take care of herself, but she'd never been up against a dozen men, and she couldn't forget Miriam and Alisa. Paul had immediately placed himself between them and the townsmen; even with a broken arm, he'd had an air of power and control she could only admire.

Her reverie was interrupted by the sound of Miriam's voice asking Gus for peppermint sticks and licorice for the girls. The whitewash she listed surprised everyone.

"You're gonna whitewash your cabin, Miriam?" Reba asked, smiling. "You'll be surprised at the difference."

Miriam nodded. "I've been wanting to for a while, now. That's it for the Chance account, Reba, but there are a few other matters to settle. I've got some eggs and butter out in the wagon."

"Butter? Nobody 'round here bothers to make it." Gus's voice betrayed his eagerness. "I can give you, say, twenty cents a pound, Miriam."

"Oh, I'd say twenty-three is fairer. We both know you'll sell it for more than that. Anyway, I've got ten bricks I can sell you, and I'll take the other nine to Mr. Scudd at the restaurant."

"I'll give you twenty-five cents a brick if you sell it all to me."

"Deal. You'll make a tidy profit when you sell it to the restaurant, too."

"We've also brought seven dozen eggs," Alisa chimed in.

Gus nodded. "I can give you twenty cents a dozen for those. It's a bit high, but nobody around here really raises chickens, and the ones as do eat their own eggs. There's plenty who will pay for 'em. Let me see, that's nineteen bricks of butter at two bits each, and seven dozen eggs at twenty cents a dozen—

that'll be six fifteen, total. Did you want cash?"

"I'll tell you what, Mr. White. Why don't you and Paul haul in the goods from the wagon while we women discuss what we'd like to do."

"I need about five yards of flannel and six of the green gingham, Reba, and a special order for baby buttons." Reba, busily writing down the order, broke her pencil.

"Did I hear that right? Did you say 'baby buttons' just as innocently as could be? You're in the family way! So that's why your cousin is here! Oh, this'll be the first babe since your sister's, God rest her soul. And you hiding it behind your cloak! You give old Reba a hug this minute!" She came around the counter and all but smothered Miriam in a jubilant embrace. She shared an amused glance with Alisa, but Delilah felt the same way Reba did. Miriam loved Hannah and Dan's girls, but she had told Delilah in her letters how much she wanted children of her own. *Maybe someday I'll finally have a family, too.*

"How far along are you? Are you feeling all right?"

"I'm doing just fine, and I expect the baby in about four months."

"Oooh. 'Four months,' she says. That means you're five along and haven't told me. Shame on you! Oh, but it doesn't matter, I'm that happy for you. Which pattern of flannel would you like?"

"The blue plaid, please."

"You've already got an inkling that your babe will be a strapping boy, do you? Small wonder when your husband has five brothers. There you are. What else can I get you?"

Miriam turned to Alisa. "We earned about three dollars each, and I've spent mine. What would you like to spend your share on?"

"I brought back everything I needed from San Francisco, but it seems to me that Delilah did an awful lot of churning. You'll need a good cape and skirt for the winter—it's never too early to think about these things. I'd say we should get some good wool."

"Wonderful idea. I thought the same thing." Miriam laughed. "We'll use most of the green gingham I'm buying for a work dress."

"No. That's your money. You should spend it on yourself, both of you." Delilah didn't want any handouts.

" 'The laborer is worthy of his hire,' the Bible tells us. You've done a lot of work on the homestead, and you'll need heavier clothing when it snows. Since the Lord blessed me with everything I need, I want you and Miriam to split it." Alisa was rapidly becoming the most generous person Delilah had ever known. If she refused the gift, it would hurt Alisa's feelings. Besides, they were telling her that they wanted her to stay through winter—that would mean a whole year here!

"All right," Delilah gave in as graciously as she could. "What will I need?"

"I'd say three yards of the gray plaid with black and red shooting through it for a skirt and about four yards of black for a good warm cape. You're tall but slender, so it will be enough," Alisa decided.

"Wool's the most expensive fabric for good reason. You'll be nice and cozy in it," Reba approved. "The seven yards comes to about two dollars' worth. What else?"

Delilah looked to Miriam and Alisa. "I'd like a charcoal pencil for my drawing and a few packets of flower seeds to plant in front of the cabin, if that's all right."

"I'd forgotten you draw, Delilah. You'll have to show me

some of the pictures you've made when we get back," Miriam exclaimed.

"What a wonderful idea! We've tried, but the place still seems more masculine than anything else. Some flowers would be welcome." Alisa's approval made Delilah decide on the spot she'd plant some in front of her new friend's cabin the moment she got a chance. For now, she had a home—and they wanted her for a whole year. She might as well enjoy it while it lasted.

six

Delilah stepped into the kitchen with four dozen eggs and a smile. She'd now been at Chance Ranch for an entire week—longer than at any residence she'd ever known. She'd come to look forward to waking up and joining Miriam and Alisa in the kitchen, where she'd learn how to make something new and delicious.

"Are we getting started on the baked apples?" She remembered promising Bryce his favorite treat.

"No. We'll make those so we can have them right after lunch. Everybody gets one, so it wouldn't be enough for breakfast." Miriam placed a towel over a bowl of dough. "This morning we'll make french toast."

"For the Lord's Day." Alisa moved a stack of thick slices toward the stove.

"Oh." Delilah felt the smile slide off her face. The Lord's Day? For Papa, that was just a day to sleep off the effects of Saturday's revelry since the saloons were closed, but she knew that wasn't how most people behaved. When she was a little girl, Mama would read from the Bible or, if the town were big enough, take her to hear a preacher. The very thought of listening to someone expound on the idea of what a sinner she was for hours on end made Delilah's stomach lurch.

"The rain's wiped away any chance of anyone coming over for the service, so the men can relax a bit instead of setting up outside the barn."

Miriam's words lifted Delilah's spirits. No preacher and a

day of relaxation didn't sound bad at all. Besides, at least for today, Paul wouldn't have to feel bad about not being able to help his brothers until his arm healed.

"What can I do to help?" Time passed quickly as she got swept up in making breakfast. Mixing eggs with cinnamon and milk, then dipping bread into the mixture before frying it to a golden brown was much easier than she'd thought it would be, and soon the men began filtering through the door, noses twitching appreciatively.

After breakfast, everyone pitched in to clean up. The table was cleared and the dishes done in record time. Surveying the sparkling kitchen, Delilah wondered what the men would do all day. Her question was answered when Gideon brought in a worn Bible and settled to the right of his usual position at the head of the table. As though the action were an unspoken command, the rest of the family flocked to join him. Reluctant to join in for reasons too numerous to count, Delilah wondered whether there was any way to excuse herself. Obviously this was a family religious gathering. Since she didn't believe as they did and couldn't count herself as a member of the family, there was no place for her here.

She watched as Paul took the seat at the head of the table, waited until everyone else was situated, and beckoned for her to sit at his left. When she hesitated, Gideon shot a glance at Miriam, who rose from her seat, walked over, and took Delilah's hand.

"Come on, it's time for worship. It's all right if you don't know the words to the hymns Titus will lead us in. Gideon will be praying for our family and friends, and Paul has chosen the scripture for today."

With that, any hope of wiggling out of this disappeared more quickly than the french toast had earlier. Pasting a smile on her face, Delilah slid onto the bench and bowed her head as Paul and Ginny Mae each held one of her hands. Clinging to the comfort of Paul's warm, steady grasp, she blinked back tears at Gideon's prayer.

"Lord, we come before you happy and whole and blessed beyond what we deserve. Right now, we know that across the world some people are not so fortunate. Please be with those who lost their homes and loved ones when Vesuvius burst open and rained fire upon the land. We know Thou art there, keeping watch over Thy children. Please help us never to lose sight of how blessed we are by Thy love. Amen."

Titus asked if anyone had any particular hymn they'd like to sing.

"I'd love to sing 'Holy, Holy, Holy,' " Alisa offered.

Delilah closed her eyes as everyone followed Titus's deep baritone. Although she tried to ignore the lyrics, instead silently reciting recipes she'd learned or what kinds of flowers she'd plant in the garden, the lovely music broke through her thoughts. She didn't want to listen because she didn't agree with what was said.

How can they think that God is "merciful and mighty"? If He really exists, He took away Mama and didn't help Papa overcome his weaknesses.

" 'Early in the morning, our song shall rise to Thee. . . .' " The words and melody were so lovely! Even Daniel's scowl faded as Polly's little voice piped in, trilling the words in slightly off-key exuberance.

After another song Delilah didn't recognize, Paul started the lesson.

"Here we sit, surrounded by friends and family in a solid home on good land. These are only a few of the blessings God has bestowed upon us. But I've been thinking about Mama and Papa a lot lately, how proud they'd be to see how much our family has grown. They built the foundation on faith and love, and it has withstood hard times. But in chasing the past, we can easily lose track of all the wonder of the present—" his eyes met hers "—and the promise of the future."

"The Bible reading is about following the Lord wherever He sees fit to lead and giving thanks for the blessings He provides, rather than looking back on things that are no more."

The lump in her throat swelled at Paul's words, and anger pulsed at her temples. *Is he talking about me? It's only right and natural to grieve when a loved one is lost!* Taking a deep breath, she listened as Paul read about a city given over entirely to sin. Only one man in the entire city found favor with God. Well, she could easily believe that. After all, as far as she could see, God was mighty selective about the people He looked after. Mama prayed and read the Bible every day and did her best to be a good wife and mother. She begged for God to help Papa stop gambling and longed for the security of a home. Instead, she died in a strange town with no money to see a doctor. If Mama, whose heart held no selfishness, wasn't good enough for God, there was precious little hope left for anyone else.

Paul read on. " 'And when the morning arose, then the angels hastened Lot, saying, Arise, take thy wife, and thy two daughters, which are here; lest thou be consumed in the iniquity of the city. . . . And it came to pass, when they had brought them forth abroad, that he said, Escape for thy life; look not behind thee. . . . ' "

Ah, so there's the part where he was talking about not thinking on the past. Comforted that Paul hadn't been pointing her out, she listened more carefully as he continued.

" 'Behold now, thy servant hath found grace in thy sight,

and thou hast magnified thy mercy, which thou hast shewed unto me in saving my life. . . .' "

Wait a minute. God saved Lot's life from whom? From Himself? That doesn't seem very benevolent. So He saves one man and destroys entire cities, and that is magnifying His mercy? Maybe there's a turn in the middle, and He saves the cities to show His mercy! Delilah listened intently to the next verses.

" 'Then the Lord rained upon Sodom and upon Gomorrah brimstone and fire from the Lord out of heaven; And he overthrew those cities, and all the plain, and all the inhabitants of the cities, and that which grew upon the ground. But his wife looked back from behind him, and she became a pillar of salt.' "

Nope. He destroyed the cities. Even Lot couldn't depend on God to protect his family. No, this God who smote entire cities and turned a woman into salt simply for watching can't be the God of love, too. It just doesn't fit. Where is the lesson here?

"So the lesson here. . . ," Paul's voice mimicked her thoughts almost exactly, "is stated by Christ Himself in Luke 17. This tale is specifically used by the Savior to remind us that we need to make Him the focus of our lives.

" 'Remember Lot's wife. Whosoever shall seek to save his life shall lose it; and whosoever shall lose his life shall preserve it.' "

That makes no sense!

"Now, this may seem to contradict itself," Paul clarified, "but Jesus isn't just talking about life as we know it, but eternal life, too. The only way to gain eternal life is by giving Christ this one."

His words sent shivers up Delilah's spine. *How can I be asked to give my life to the control of someone when everyone I've depended on has let me down?*

"Once we acknowledge God as the one who created us and give ourselves to Him, we will live forever in His grace. Let's pray."

Thoughts whirled through Delilah's head as the family joined hands once more. *How could anyone live forever? It just isn't possible.* She'd seen death in all its horrible finality—no one could escape the threat that came and stole all smiles and laughter and life.

Mama gave her life to Jesus. How can I trust Him when He took Mama away and didn't save her? And how can I tell these people who believe in salvation they're wrong when I don't understand it? Why do they have the same peace and joy in God that Mama had? Delilah's heart ached as the others sang another hymn she didn't recognize. *Why can't I understand what they believe and be as happy as they are? What am I missing?*

Her thoughts came to a halt as she recognized the melody everyone sang. As the words poured forth, Delilah remembered the hymn as one of her mother's favorites. Despite her resolution not to take part, she mouthed the words:

"Blest be the tie that binds
Our hearts in Christian love. . ."

She snuck at glance at Paul, only to find him watching her. At his encouraging nod, she raised her voice and joined in:

"The fellowship of kindred minds
Is like to that above."

Amidst the deep voices of the brothers around her, Delilah could almost hear her mother's clear soprano. By the third verse, she blinked back tears at the memory.

It was no use. God had abandoned her long ago, and there was no tie to bind her to these good people, no matter how much she wished for one. At least there was one thing she could take away from Paul's lesson. She didn't have to keep reliving the past and regretting what she couldn't change. Instead, she'd focus on these people who opened their home and hearts to her. For now.

❧

Paul smiled as he remembered the service that morning. His lovely little lady couldn't carry a tune in a bucket, but somehow that added to her charm. After all, no one was perfect. And if he wasn't mistaken, the Lord had begun answering his prayer about softening her heart to the truth. He'd watched her reaction to the hymns and the Bible reading and seen a woman lost in deep thought and longing. It was too much to think she'd already come completely to God, but the seed was planted. *Thank You, Father.*

"Hey! It's your turn, Paul!" Titus called.

Logan waved a horseshoe as his brother walked across the barn.

"If I were you, I wouldn't be so eager to lose first place," Paul joked.

"What?" Logan joined in the good-natured ribbing. "I know you always said you could beat us with one hand tied behind your back, but I never thought to see it tested!"

Paul stifled a groan as he remembered his arrogant boast from last month. He hadn't expected to have to prove it! Pulling his good arm back, he tossed the horseshoe at the spike, only opening his eyes when he heard a promising clang.

"Well, I'll be." Gideon laughed. "I reckon he was right, after all. Don't suppose you'd care to repeat that performance?"

"What, and lose my moment of victory?" Paul protested.

"Nope. I think I'll just stroll inside for some cool water and see how supper is coming along." He headed for the house, ignoring the taunts aimed at him by his brothers about how he just didn't think he could make that shot twice in a row.

Truthfully, he probably couldn't. But he had a powerful thirst to quench. He opened the door to a mix of tantalizing smells.

"Need some water?" Miriam handed him a cupful.

"How's supper coming along? Smells good enough in here to tempt the angels."

"We just put the roast in the oven. The biscuits are rising and the apples are ready for baking, but we'll put them in later so they don't get cold." Alisa smiled. "Did Titus put you up to throwing horseshoes regardless of your arm?"

Holding back a grin at how well Alisa knew her husband, Paul tried to think of an answer that wouldn't get them both in trouble.

"Just one to defend my place. Besides, it's not my throwing arm."

"I warned you to take it easy!" Miriam chided, but she couldn't hide the laughter in her tone. "You'd think first place in an ongoing horseshoes competition wouldn't be as important as your health."

"Are you all right?" Delilah gently adjusted his sling, her fingers brushing his forearm when she made sure his sleeve was still rolled up. He knew she meant to keep his sling as dry as possible in the rainy weather, but the heat following her touch succeeded more than she knew.

"Fine." He turned to Polly to mask the gruffness of his voice. "What do you have there, baby girl?"

"Lilah's going to teach me a game!" She held up a pack of cards.

"Cards?" He raised an eyebrow.

"I said it would be fine to have a hand of Old Maid," Miriam cut in. "Would you like to join Delilah and Polly? I'm sure Polly would love to have you on her team."

"I got Uncle Paul!" Polly crowed, then her face fell. "But who have you got, Lilah?"

He saw a flash of sadness cross Delilah's face and knew she thought about her parents again. He stepped in. "Ginny Mae, of course. Come on and take a seat."

Delilah had Ginny Mae on her lap and held the cards, taking out all the queens but one. She held up the remaining female face card. "All right, Polly. This is the Old Maid. Every other card has a match—fours go together, nines go together, and so on. You want to find a match to all of your cards because the first one who does, wins. The Old Maid doesn't have a match, though, so whoever has her in their hand at the end of the game loses, all right?"

"Okay. How do we get the matches?" Polly's tiny brow furrowed in serious concentration as she dangled her feet off the edge of the bench.

"First, I'm going to split the cards." Delilah dealt the hand. "Now, you need to look at your deck with Uncle Paul and take out all the matches while Ginny Mae and I do the same thing."

There was silence as Paul helped Polly match cards while Delilah's partner helpfully stuck peas in the box with the extra queens and waved it in the air.

"I gotta question. What if we got three cards that are the same number? Like these?" She held up two sixes and a nine.

"Well, honey, that's close, but not quite. Do you remember how Auntie Miriam's been teaching you numbers? Well, you haven't gotten to these yet, but a six looks like an upside-down nine. See?" He turned the cards for her inspection.

"Oh." Polly nodded sagely, her braids bouncing. "That's why there's more spots on this one, right?"

He and Delilah shared grins over that astute observation as Polly waved the nine of clubs.

"Right. But see, here we have three fours. So we'll take out the two with the same color," he plunked two down on the table, "and keep this one until we get another four. Got it?"

"Got it." Polly beamed at him. "We got rid of lots of cards, so," she lowered her voice, "we're gonna win, right? 'Cuz we don't have the one with the lady on it?"

"That's where it gets tricky," Paul warned. "See, Delilah should have the same numbers of cards we do, so we have to pick one from her to try and make another match. But if we pick the Old Maid, and we still have it by the end, we'll lose. Are you ready?"

Polly stretched across the table toward Delilah's hand, and the game began. The Old Maid traveled from team to team until finally, Polly sat with one card while Delilah held two.

"All right, Polly. You've got to pick one. We're looking for a two, but if you get the Old Maid, Delilah might still win."

Polly grasped a card and turned it around. "We won, Uncle Paul! Look! Lilah's an o—old ma—aid, Lilah's the o—old ma—aid," she singsonged, then stopped suddenly to tug on his sleeve. "Whatsa old maid?"

"Well. . ." Paul was at a loss for words.

"It's a lady who's not married even though she's been old enough to be for a while, Polly." Delilah's tremulous smile twisted something inside him.

"So you really *are* an old maid!" Delighted, Polly scooted off the bench to go tell Miriam.

"No, you aren't," Paul stated firmly, holding Delilah's gaze.

"Yes, I am. It's all right," she assured him as she picked up Ginny Mae and went after Polly.

Not for long, if the Lord's will and mine are the same.

seven

Later that week, Delilah looked at the small plot of land she and Paul had been working on. Together, they'd watered the soil for three days before Logan and Bryce could hoe it up easily and turn the dirt to let in air. Her nose wrinkled at the memory of the fertilizer they'd used the previous morning.

Today would make it all worthwhile. Today they'd finally begin planting the seeds and bulbs.

I wonder whether I'll be here long enough to see them bloom. I hope so. It will be beautiful next year with all those colors. And Polly and Ginny Mae want to help me water and weed. They may pull up the plants when they begin sprouting, so I'll have to teach them which ones are flowers.

Delilah went to her cabin to fetch the flower seeds. She stepped around the cabin to find Paul playing patty-cake with the girls. Ginny Mae followed the pattern as Polly sat in Paul's lap and tried to fill in for his left arm. As giggles floated through the air, Delilah's breath caught at the homey scene.

"No, Uncle Paul. You forgot this one!" Polly gestured in the air.

Delilah let loose a peal of laughter at Paul's abashed expression, catching everyone's attention. His handsome face broke into a grin.

"Looks like Delilah's here just in time to save me from any more mistakes." He stood up. "Are you ready to plant the flowers?"

"Yea!" Polly grabbed Ginny Mae's hand, and they both raced toward the garden.

Paul fell in step beside Delilah. "Have you decided where you want everything?"

The humor in his tone almost made her blush. She'd written lists of every kind of flower they had, then sketched where she would plant each variety. She'd taken some jokes about how many times she'd changed her mind but knew they meant no harm by it. Honestly, there were so many things to consider! She didn't want to clump all of the same color together but instead wanted to spread them out so it looked like a rainbow touched the earth. Also, some of the flowers would bloom in different months, and she couldn't leave patches bare while others sprang in glorious blossoms.

Maybe she was going a bit overboard, but the Chances just couldn't understand why she wanted this garden to be absolutely perfect. Even after she left, this garden should stay beautiful, a lasting testament that she'd made a difference somewhere.

"I think so." Delilah smiled up at Paul, the only person who'd been patient enough to help her throughout her quest. Well, Miriam had helped her know when each plant would blossom, but Paul spent hours helping her remove all the rocks and prepare the land. He'd actually chosen the plot for having plenty of sunlight with adequate protection against winter winds. His smile and able advice helped make this project such a joy. Not that she knew how to tell him!

"Do you have the markers?" His deep voice broke into her thoughts.

"Right here." She brandished the small pieces of wood on which she'd painstakingly written the name of each flower she would plant. The clever folding desk in her room had been much used lately.

"All right. I've numbered each stick, and here's a little map for where each number goes, so the flowers will be planted there." The morning whirled by as Paul helped Ginny Mae dig shallow holes while Polly practiced her numbers counting out seeds to drop inside. Delilah gently dusted them again with dirt.

"What will these look like?" Polly's oft-repeated question let Delilah describe the pretty flowers.

"From March to May, we'll see white evening primroses and blue wild hyacinths," she described, pointing to the areas where they'd planted the seeds. "April will bring lavender godetias, spring beauties, and live forever."

"Like we're going to in heaben?" Ginny Mae's question sent pangs through Delilah's heart. How could she explain now that a flower called live forever didn't really live forever—and neither could she.

"That's right, ladybug." Paul stepped in. "In a lot of ways, flowers are just like we are. They need food and water and sunshine and love and all the good things God made for us. But you won't always be able to see the flowers. You have to know that they bloom and fade away, but they make seeds. See, that's the really important part that makes it so this special flower can bloom again later."

Polly frowned in concentration. "So how's that like us? You can always see me."

"Do you remember what we told you about heaven, Polly?"

"Yes, it's a beautiful place where I'll see Mommy again, and we'll live forever with Jesus!" Her face brightened.

"Do you remember how you have to leave here first?" At the little girl's nod, he continued. "It's just the same as this flower. See, Mommy faded away and left here, but her soul, just like the seeds, is made of something stronger, and it's that part that goes to heaven and makes it so we'll see her again if we believe in Jesus."

" 'Cuz she had Jesus in her heart," Polly finished, taking her sister's hand.

Tears pricked Delilah's eyes as she watched the tender scene. If all that was true—and she was by no means certain it was—then Mama would be in heaven because she believed in Christ. *But I won't be there to see her because I can't believe.* The helplessness of it all washed over her in a suffocating wave. Paul's words from the day before echoed in her mind. "The only way to gain eternal life is by giving Christ this one."

Polly's voice interrupted her thoughts. "We can't 'member Mama, but she loves us, Ginny Mae."

"Jesus gots Mama," Ginny Mae stated firmly, then reached up to tug on the end of Polly's braid. "Daddy gots us."

Delilah's heart ached. *Jesus has my mama, too.*

"Yep. And we've got lotsa people: Uncle Paul, Uncle Titus, Uncle Logan, Uncle Bryce, Auntie Miriam, Auntie Alisa—" Polly grabbed Paul's hand.

"And Lilah, too." Ginny Mae grabbed a handful of Delilah's dress.

Touched at the little girl's gesture, Delilah smiled. "We've all got each other," she agreed.

"And now we're gonna have flowers." Polly brushed some dirt over another batch of bulbs. "So what'll these be?"

"Those will be mariposa lilies. They'll be white, and we'll see them in May with the daisies."

"What color are daisies?"

"They'll be white or yellow. I don't know which!" Delilah confessed. "These'll be wild roses. I don't know what color they'll be, either. The dog roses over here will be pink like the end of Ginny Mae's nose when she's cold." Polly smiled at that, and Delilah pressed on. "The saxifrages are tiny white bunches of flowers that we'll see around the same time. After those, in July or so, the larkspurs will come—they're white and blue. The last flowers to stay will be the red farewell-to-springs, and then we'll have to wait until the next year to plant them again."

"That oughta do it." Paul stepped back and surveyed their handiwork. The bell jangled from the kitchen. "And just in time for lunch, too." He deftly swiped a wriggling worm from Ginny Mae's pudgy grasp and scooped her into his arms.

"Let's go get washed up." Polly slipped her hand into Delilah's and marched toward the house.

Delilah dipped a rag in the washbasin and bent down to wipe Polly's hands and face.

"I can do it," Polly protested, tugging the makeshift wash-cloth away from Delilah. "But you can help Uncle Paul." She gestured toward the washstand with the towel, flinging drops of water down the front of Delilah's dress.

"All right." Suppressing a smile at how quickly little Polly was growing up, Delilah turned to find Paul bouncing Ginny Mae with his good arm. Delilah grabbed another rag to clean Ginny Mae.

"Impressive amount of dirt for such a tiny thing, isn't it?" Paul's voice rumbled with good humor as Delilah grimaced at the dirty towel.

"I'll say. If we covered the seeds with this much, they'd never make it to the surface!"

"Daddy!" Polly skipped to the door as Daniel walked in. Ginny Mae wiggled and held out her arms.

"Hello sugar-dumpling. Let me wash up a minute." He affectionately rumpled her hair.

A few moments later, everyone was gathered at the table. Looking around, Delilah marveled at the fact she knew each and every name and face around her. A sense of contentment at the familiarity of joining hands to say grace washed away her discomfort at the religious practice. She almost felt like family. Out of the corner of her eye, she saw Titus give Alisa's hand one last squeeze before letting go. The obvious comfort they found in one another tugged at Delilah's heart.

Will I ever share that closeness with someone?

"Of course." Paul's deep voice startled her.

Hope and horror warred within her as she stammered, "I—I beg your pardon?"

"Logan asked if you'd like some biscuits, and I said, 'of course.' " He smiled as he held the basket for her. "There you go."

"Thanks." She somehow managed a smile as she grabbed one of Miriam's warm, flaky biscuits, her heart still thumping wildly. She was grateful when Alisa spoke, drawing Paul's attention.

"Tomorrow morning before you men set off, we'd appreciate if you'd help move the furniture in Gideon and Miriam's cabin so we can whitewash it."

"Sure," Bryce agreed immediately.

"If the weather's fine," Daniel conceded.

"Are you going to need an extra hand, Paul?" Logan offered.

"Delilah and I'll manage just fine." She liked the way he said her name. Paul had a way of making ordinary things seem more beautiful than they really were.

And that's exactly why I have to be careful. A man like Paul could put a woman's head in the clouds, thinking they made a castle. But come the next strong wind, they'd blow away and she'd be left with nothing. Better to enjoy what was than to put stock in dreams.

❧

The next day, the women bustled over to the cabin Miriam and Gideon shared. Working as quickly as possible, they removed all clothing from the pegs as well as the small mirror hung above the dresser, baring the walls and taking anything they could from the room. They stored it all in Delilah's cabin, which she'd share with Miriam until the smell from the whitewash stopped lingering.

"There. That ought to do it." Miriam's pronouncement came just in time as the brothers filed in, effectively crowding what had seemed a generous space scant moments before.

"So you're finished?" Gideon gestured to the now-bare walls.

"We've taken everything we possibly could," Alisa confirmed.

"Would you look at that!" Bryce stood beside the small dresser. "They even took the drawers out!"

Titus let loose an amused guffaw. Perplexed, Delilah looked at Paul, only to see him exchange grins with Logan.

"What's so funny?"

"Don't you women think that, with all six of us, we could've moved it even with the drawers inside?" It was the first time Delilah saw Daniel smile without his daughters around.

"We knew you could handle it." Miriam put a hand on Alisa's back and steered her, spluttering, from the room. "It's better for the furniture this way. We'll just leave you to remove the heavy pieces."

Delilah followed, glad to see that everyone was comfortable enough with her around to act like a real family—tiffs, teasing, and all. Next thing she knew, she stood in the empty room next to Paul.

"Ever whitewashed before, Delilah?"

"No, but I know my way around a paintbrush." She thought of her precious paint set, safely tucked away in her cabin. Maybe she could start teaching Polly to sketch. . .if Daniel would let her and they had the time. But for now, there was work to be done.

"Have you?" She hoped he had. There were sure to be differences between watercolor strokes and wall painting.

"Long time ago. When I was a lad, Mama, my brothers, and I did the outside of our house."

His wistful smile twisted her heart. "That's the first time I've heard you mention your mother, aside from Sunday," Delilah said softly.

"Yeah, well, she was a wonderful woman—godly and loving and generous. She passed on soon after we made Chance Ranch our home." He visibly straightened as he changed the topic. "First you stir it to make sure the color's blended." Looking up to make sure she was watching, he caught her smile before she could hide it.

"What?"

"Nothing. I was just thinking that's probably about how I look when I'm tending the stew." She needn't have worried he'd be offended.

He gave a grin. "Just about, but I'm nowhere near as pretty, and I hope you never have to try my cooking. I'll just leave it to you."

Warmth filled her cheeks at the compliment, so she turned away to pick up the large paintbrushes. "So we're just coating the walls, right?"

"Yep. No point in doing the floor white—it'd just get dirty faster. And we could do the ceiling, but it'd drip on the furniture." He gestured to the middle of the room, where they'd piled everything.

"So where do we start?" Suddenly the room looked immense.

"We each take a wall. You're going to want to paint along with the wood grain, side to side, otherwise it'll drip down and not look as nice as we want it."

"All right." Delilah dipped her brush and went to a wall. "Like this?"

"Not quite. You want to have a longer stroke." He held her elbow and guided her arm, sending tingles up and down her spine. She pulled away. "I see." To cover the awkwardness of the movement, she pointed to the top of the wall. "But I don't see how I'll manage to reach all the way up there."

"Don't expect you to. I'll get the highest parts. It'll probably be best for me to take care of that first, and then you follow." He grabbed a brush and got going.

Discomfited by his nearness, Delilah focused her entire concentration on the task at hand rather than on starting a conversation. What good would it do to learn more about him? He didn't complain when he broke his arm, loved his brothers, worked hard, spent time with his nieces, and spoke tenderly of his mother. He was a family man and obviously needed to find a wife who could give him as much as he gave to everyone else.

Why couldn't you do that? her heart whispered. She shook the thought away. It would never work. Sure, he was a wonderful man, but he was still just that—a man. If she let herself fall for him and marry him, he'd have the right to make her go anywhere he liked. She just couldn't take the risk.

eight

The hours passed in a deep silence Paul wasn't about to break. No whitewashing ever inspired a furrowed brow, so he stayed convinced Delilah was doing some deep thinking. He sure needed to.

It had been a mistake to touch her arm. Despite the long sleeve on her dress, his fingertips still sizzled at the memory of that contact. She'd felt it, too, since she'd abruptly pulled away, skittish as a frightened colt. Maybe she was thinking about what it meant. The question certainly plagued him.

Lord, why do I feel so deeply for this woman if it isn't Thy will? How can I help her see Thy hand in the beautiful things she loves? I understand why she's afraid to trust others, but not all of it. Please, Lord, give me the strength not to hand her my heart until she gives hers to Thee. And give us both the time we need.

They finished the last bare patch, and Delilah stepped back to survey their handiwork. "That went faster than I thought it would." She offered a tentative smile.

Grateful for the gesture, Paul grinned back. "Good company can conquer time."

As her cheeks turned pink for the second time that day, he decided her inability to accept a compliment only added to her charm.

To his surprise, she didn't busy herself with something.

"It's not often you can be around another person without having to fill the time with words," he observed.

"I know what you mean," she said softly.

His heart thumped as she agreed. This meant she was becoming more comfortable around him.

They gathered their brushes and walked out to the pump. She held the brushes under the water while he pumped. The hot and dusty day alone couldn't account for the dust cloud they spotted in the distance.

"That's odd. Miriam hasn't rung the dinner bell yet, and your brothers are already coming home. I hope everything's all right."

Paul wondered whether she remembered the day he'd broken his arm and worried for his brothers.

"Wait a minute. They wouldn't be coming from the east. Wonder what would bring someone out on a Saturday?" He shaded his eyes and squinted as the wagon came closer. As soon as he realized the approaching horses carried the MacPherson brothers, he tried to get Delilah in the house. Why else would they come a day before they should for worship—unless they were coming courting.

"Delilah, why don't you go tell Miriam we might be having company for dinner?"

"All right." She cast one last look over her shoulder and headed for the kitchen.

Paul started walking out to meet them. Maybe he could find out what they needed and send them away without letting them so much as get a glimpse of Delilah.

Mike pulled up beside him. "Reckoned we was a-mite late fer the doin's. Hadda hole smack dab in one a th' fences."

It took Paul a moment to realize they thought it was Sunday, and by then, Obie had chimed in.

"Yeah, and seein's how the gully-washer kept us away week afore today, we figgered we'uns best try an come anyhow."

"Gentlemen," Paul interrupted, "I'm afraid there's been a mistake. You're a day early. Tomorrow is the Lord's Day." Maybe he could get them to turn around and go home before Miriam rang the dinner bell.

"Aw, you're joshin' us fer shore. Leave off cuttin' up." Hezzy guffawed, but Micah silently counted on his fingers.

"Naw, he ain't! Think on it, Hezekiah MacPherson." Micah glared at his older brother, who scratched his head in bewilderment.

"You're the only one as can cipher, Mike. I reckon ya musta messed up." It seemed as though Obie's well-meaning intervention hadn't helped.

"If'n I done tole ya once, I tole ya agin an' agin. Ya mark the day off after dark! If'n ya cross it off of a mornin', we end up a day ahead 'cuz this one ain't o'er yet!"

Hezekiah had the grace to look abashed. "Shore am sorry, Mike. I done fergot agin."

Paul watched the brothers confer until he couldn't wait any longer to get them out of there. After all, once the dinner bell rang, it would be too late to get them to leave.

"Well, if it isn't the MacPherson brothers!" Paul winced as Miriam bustled up.

"Ma'am." Mike respectfully tipped his grimy hat, and his brothers mimicked the gesture.

"Why are you out in the hot sun? Dinner'll be on the table soon. Come on in."

"We don' wanna be botherin' ya, but we shore would be tickled to sample some of those fine vittles o' yourn, ma'am." The three of them beamed down at Miriam even as Paul quelled the urge to glare at all four of them.

What is she thinking? Paul watched helplessly as they all

hopped out of the wagon and followed Miriam.

≈

Delilah dropped the edge of the curtain as Miriam headed toward the house. She recognized the three men as ones they'd seen at the general store but didn't quite understand why Paul seemed so displeased to see them. Two were large bears of men, but the third stood shorter and had a wiry build. One thing was clear: They would be staying for dinner. Delilah quickly slid three more bowls on the table as Miriam rang the dinner bell. The men strode inside.

"Delilah, you may remember the MacPherson brothers: Obadiah, Hezekiah, and Micah," Miriam said in introduction

Obie spoke up. "Aw, no need ta stand on ceremony with us. We's just plain Obie, Hezzy, and Mike."

"He's got the right of it," Hezzy added. "Don't make a lick a sense to call us all 'Mr. MacPherson.'"

"Right nice to make your aquaintanceship, miss." Mike bowed over her hand.

"Aw, wouldja look at the jack-a-dandy come a-courtin'," one of the older brothers crowed.

"Hush your face, Obie," Hezzy whispered loudly as he elbowed his brother.

"Pleasure to meet you," Delilah greeted them, amused rather than appalled by their manners. They seemed well-meaning enough, after all. She didn't like the reference to courting, but the thought that this was the reason Paul seemed so put out lifted her spirits.

"What're you doin' here?" Daniel growled as he stepped up to the washbasin.

Delilah was relieved to see that the MacPhersons didn't seem to take offense at Daniel's curt tone.

"We swapped days, I reckon," Obie explained, then seemed

struck by an unwelcome thought. He turned to Mike, clearly the brains of the family. "We kin still come tomorra, right?"

Hezzy's face fell at that, and the pair of them looked for all the world like children about to be denied a treat.

Mike nodded. "We still gotta honor the Lord's Day."

The older brothers broke out in matching grins. As Paul scowled at the blue willow plate Miriam loaded with biscuits, Delilah bit back a smile of her own.

nine

Everyone began jockeying for a seat. Paul noticed the MacPherson brothers hovering around the table as though waiting for Delilah to sit down so they could swoop in beside her.

His eyes narrowed. Over his dead body would they get any closer to her than absolutely necessary. He plunked down toward the end of the bench and snagged Delilah as she leaned over to put another batch of biscuits on the table. The second he was certain he had a hold of her, he hooked his boot around her foot to make her stumble right onto the seat beside him.

"Oh! Sorry, I must've tripped." She made as if to get up, but he didn't let go of her arm.

"I've never known you to be clumsy. You'd best stay seated—sometimes the smell from the whitewash can make a person lightheaded."

"Just stay put, Delilah," Miriam said with a slight wink toward Paul. "We're just about done, anyway."

Maybe Miriam was trying to make amends for inviting the MacPhersons to lunch. Whatever the reason, he'd be glad for any help she'd give him.

There was a brief tussle as Obie and Hezzy both tried to elbow their way to the end of the bench. Hezzy won and got there first. Fortunately, try as he might, he couldn't figure out a way to squeeze his large frame onto the half inch of bench peeking out by Delilah's skirts.

"Ahem," the big oaf cleared his throat. "I'd be much obliged if'n ya could see your way clear ta scoochin' o'er a bit, miss. Don't much fancy perchin' like a jaybird durin' vittles."

His bumbling manners coaxed a smile from Delilah as she obligingly began scooting over. Paul didn't move, which he found yielded double benefits: Firstly, it stopped Hezzy from sitting down, and secondly, Delilah was now close enough that Paul could catch the scent of jasmine that lingered sweetly in her hair.

"If it's all the same to you, Hezzy, I'd appreciate it if you'd try the other bench. If we're packed tighter than a tin of sardines, my arm'll give me trouble." Paul avoided looking across the table at Daniel, who sat parked next to Obie already.

"Oh, how thoughtless of me!" Delilah interjected. "Paul's been working hard whitewashing, and it certainly won't help to have Logan jostling his arm today, too. Do you mind?"

Paul was gratified to hear the concern in her voice as she neatly made it impossible for Hezzy to refuse.

"Yes'm." Hezzy shuffled over to the other bench, where Polly obligingly bounced over toward her father. Hezzy hunkered down, and the bench gave an ominous creak.

Obie snatched a biscuit and crammed the whole thing in his mouth while the Chance family joined hands. Paul supposed Micah kicked his brother under the table, because Obie let loose with, "Ow," spraying his plate and beard with crumbs before catching on and bowing his head for prayer.

"Wait, that hurts!"

Paul looked over at Hezzy to see him pinching Polly's tiny hand between his forefinger and thumb.

"Open your hand," she ordered, and the giant obeyed without question. Polly placed her hand in the middle of his palm, then used her other hand to fold Hezzy's fingers over, completely engulfing her hand and wrist. "See, like this." Satisfied, she tucked her other hand back in Ginny Mae's and nodded. "We're ready now, Uncle Gideon."

Smiling, Gideon closed his eyes and blessed the food before he began ladling the thick venison stew into bowls and passing them down either side of the table. Hezzy grabbed the bowl, looked at it longingly, and tried to give it to Polly before Daniel swiped it from him.

Sitting at the other end of the table, Mike received his stew first.

"Watcha waitin' fer?" Obie demanded, indignant to see the untouched meal.

"Is good manners ta wait fer everyone else," Mike growled, trying to keep his voice down but failing miserably nevertheless.

"Oh." Crumbs sprinkled from his beard as Obie nodded sagely.

The moment everyone was served, the three brothers picked up their bowls and tipped them to their mouths, downing the stew as quickly as possible.

Everyone else watched in a kind of morbid fascination when all three plunked their empty bowls back on the table. Micah wiped his mouth with his sleeve while Obie and Hezzy made short work of their biscuits. Only when Obie let loose a satisfied sigh scant moments later did they realize no one else had so much as touched their meal.

Micah and Obie seemed uncomfortable, while Hezzy eyed Polly's biscuits greedily. "Ya gonna et this 'ere extry biskit?" He poked the bread with a grimy finger.

Wordlessly, Polly pushed the biscuit toward him, head cocked to the side as she watched him bring it up to his mouth. Then, Hezzy caught Alisa staring at him, eyes agog.

"Wha's happenin'?"

No one knew quite how to answer that question. To be honest, Paul didn't mind the way things were turning out. At least they finished sooner, so they'd leave more quickly.

"How come you eat like that?" Polly asked, only to receive blank looks from the MacPhersons.

"They's hungwy!" Ginny Mae piped up.

"Shore are." Mike latched on to the little girl's assessment. "We bin livin' offa Obie's victuals for nigh on half a year now. Almost fergot how real food tastes."

"Maybe that's 'cuz you don't chew." No one knew quite what to do about Polly's helpful suggestion until Mike burst out laughing.

"Reckon tha' might be so, missy," he choked out as his brothers joined in, giving great guffaws. Relieved, the rest of the table gave way to amused chuckles.

"Would you like seconds?" The words were hardly out of Miriam's mouth before the brothers thrust their bowls toward her.

"Use your spoon!" Polly said.

Hezzy picked up one of the spoons, dwarfing it in his huge fist. "I never ken why a body would wanna warsh more dishes. Food's just as good without 'em, so why bother?"

Polly had to think on that for a minute. "So's you don't spill." She reached up her napkin and wiped some soup off of Hezzy's face.

Micah slurped down his first bite and beamed as he plunged his spoon in for a second. Hezzy got his up to his mouth until it clacked against his teeth. Startled by the noise, he dropped his spoon and bent down to pick it up.

"Would you like me to clean that for you?" Delilah offered.

"Naw, what fer?" He rubbed it on the front of his shirt before trying again.

When everyone had their fill, the meal was over. Paul felt pretty satisfied with how he'd handled things. After all, not one of the three brothers had sat beside her or even talked to her directly. To the contrary, they'd fallen on the food like animals and done serious damage if they thought they'd convince Delilah to be their bride.

"Got lotta work ta git ta back home. Can't hardly wait 'til tomorra." Micah once again served as the spokesman for the group as his older brothers nodded in tandem and patted their full bellies. With that, they got up, strode outside, unhitched the horse, and made for home in their wagon.

"So tomorrow the entire town comes over?"

Under any other circumstances, Paul would be unhappy to see Delilah's discomfiture, but here it signified her lack of interest in other men.

"Yes," Alisa confirmed. "So, since you're done whitewashing, maybe you can help me. We'll need half a dozen pies and more loaves of bread." Alisa turned to Paul. "Would you mind getting the barn as ready as you can in case it sprinkles and we need to set up inside?"

Paul went to the barn and grabbed a rake. One-handed, it wasn't easy to clear the floor, but it gave him plenty of time to think. What was he supposed to do when every man in the county would find his way over to sniff around Delilah's skirts?

Lord, give me patience, temperance, and a few good ideas!

❧

Delilah stretched before Miriam began helping with her buttons.

"Busy day, wasn't it?" Delilah could hear her cousin's smile even if she couldn't see it.

"I thought so," Delilah confessed hesitantly. "But you just

don't know how wonderful it is to have every day filled up. When I was with Papa, I'd paint or embroider to pass the time, but I haven't touched a paintbrush since I got here. I'm not exactly sure how to explain it, but planting the garden, cooking, cleaning, watching the girls, whitewashing. . .it makes me feel. . ."

"Useful?" Miriam offered.

"Yes." Delilah turned around and looked her cousin in the eye, trying to put into words what she felt. "But it's more than that. I feel like a part of something bigger than myself. Does that even make sense?"

"Of course! You're a part of a family now. And you're learning everything so quickly, you have a lot to be a part of. I'm so glad God brought you to us, Delilah." Miriam folded her into a cozy hug.

"You've done so much for me," Delilah whispered.

"It goes both ways. All of those things you've listed are of such great help. I do hope, though, we'll find some time for you to pull out those paintbrushes again!" Miriam scanned the room, seeing the drawers and pegs and quilts she'd brought in. "Where do you keep them?" she wondered aloud.

"In here." Delilah walked over to the washstand and opened the drawer. "Everything I owned that wasn't clothes or my pistol is in here. It's my entire life in one drawer." She pulled out her paint set along with her sketchbook.

Miriam sat down on the bed and ran her fingers over the much-washed tips of the brushes. "So many colors." She picked up the sketchbook. "May I?" At Delilah's nod, she started flipping through the pages, gazing at the charcoal drawings. "You've been so many places! Trains, ships, mountains, fields, wildflowers. . .and you make them all so beautiful!"

"I've seen a lot of things." Delilah didn't bother to keep the sadness from her voice. "But I haven't ever really been any-place until now. I want to paint Chance Ranch someday."

"Oh, that would be wonderful. After the baby, I can show you the fishing hole and some of the wildflowers—my favor-ite places to think and pray. You should draw one for every season! That'd keep you busy for a while longer!" Miriam smiled. "Do you ever draw people, Delilah?"

"No." Delilah looked away. There had been no one special to paint except Mama and Papa. Some of her favorite memo-ries were of Mama teaching her how to paint. They'd started on houses and flowers, full of little shapes to be painted.

The one time Delilah painted a portrait, it was of her father and mother, done from memory. Oh, how she'd slaved over it, hours upon hours, making sure the sketch was perfect before mixing the exact shade of Mama's burnished mahogany locks and Papa's black whiskers. When she'd finally finished, she'd proudly held it up for Mama's inspection. But Mama's delight faded quickly into tears.

At Delilah's confusion, Mama took out another portrait and snuggled next to Delilah. "See, baby. This is your papa right before we were married." But this man with his smooth young face and bright eyes was hardly recognizable in the lined face and tired eyes Delilah had depicted in great detail. "He's changed so much," Mama whispered, tears trickling down her face as she pressed the portrait into Delilah's hand. "Remember him this way, darling." With that, she bustled out of the room, and Delilah furiously painted over her portrait in thick black strokes. She'd never painted another person and told herself she never would.

But how to explain this now to Miriam? "I prefer to paint landscapes. Mama always said things were easier to see and understand than people." Certain Miriam would question her tired smile, Delilah changed the subject.

"What about you? What did you have when you came to Chance Ranch?"

"I brought my clothes, a Bible, a cross one of my island friends made for me, my sewing kit, writing desk, and a present I never had the chance to give my sister." Now Delilah wasn't the only one swept away by memories of loved ones gone. Miriam knelt by a small trunk. She pulled out a tiny bundle wrapped in cotton.

"This should have been Hannah's. One day, it will go to her daughters. I suppose we both brought things we haven't used." Miriam handed the package to Delilah. The loose material fell away from a small wooden box. She opened the tiny hinges to find the inside glowing with mother of pearl inlay.

"This is beautiful," she breathed.

"Oh, that's just a teakwood box. Actually, the earrings were for Hannah," Miriam explained.

Delilah unwrapped another strip of cotton to reveal large pearls set in golden earbobs. "They're lovely, and pearls like these are so rare!"

"Not on the islands!" Miriam laughed. "But here they'd fetch a fancy price. I hope to have them reset in rings or pendants for the girls." She gently wrapped everything up again and tucked the treasure in her trunk, then came back and clasped Delilah's hands.

"Lord, we thank Thee for Thy love and blessings and pray Thou wilt keep Thy hand on our loved ones. Thank Thee for friends, family, and all we hold dear. Jesus, Thou knowest what's deep in our hearts, how part of us misses our parents and always will. Please provide us with comfort while we're away from those we love and help us to remember they live in

Thee. Let us not hide behind grief or loneliness, but instead concentrate on loving each other. In Christ's name, Amen."

The words spoke to Delilah, and for the first time, she truly hoped a prayer would be answered.

ten

The sun shone brightly with nary a cloud in the sky. *So why do I feel so cold?* Delilah shivered as she listened to Gideon speak on a passage from the book of Hebrews.

Why is it that every time someone reads from the Bible, it seems as though they're talking directly to me? Phrases kept jumping out at her. "Today if ye will hear his voice, Harden not your hearts. . . . Take heed, brethren, lest there be in any of you an evil heart of unbelief, in departing from the living God. But exhort one another daily. . .lest any of you be hardened through the deceitfulness of sin."

Between nighttime devotions and sermons on the Lord's Day—not to mention constant prayers—Delilah felt surrounded by pressure to believe as these wonderful people did.

And for a change, it seemed as though she were one of the few people actually "fixing her thoughts" on the Lord this morning.

Everyone in the township had turned out, and she would have had to be deaf and blind not to realize the vast majority of people were staring at her.

Well, so long as they don't try to talk to me or touch me or anything, I'll be just fine. As they stood for another hymn, she heard a peculiar sound amidst the music.

Why won't men carry handkerchiefs when they need them? Delilah's back stiffened as the sound grew louder. Honestly, it was right behind her now.

She heard a muffled yelp and turned her head.

"You're not gonna do that ag'in, ya hear?" Mike MacPherson growled as he tightened his hold on another man's collar. "Ya jist don' go 'round sniffin' ladies. And durin' preachin'." He scoffed and released the man, who turned around as though spoiling for a good fight, only to take a small step back as Obie and Hezzy moved closer to their younger brother. He mumbled something unintelligible, shot Delilah a sheepish grin, and realized he'd become the focus of everyone's attention.

"Let us pray." Gideon quickly ended the sermon, allowing the women to escape to the kitchen. Widow Greene took the little girls and her son, Davie, out to the play yard. Priscilla White flounced along behind her, steering clear of the kitchen.

As soon as the door shut, Alisa burst into giggles. Miriam and Reba looked at Delilah with concern until she joined Alisa, and soon the entire kitchen rang with laughter.

"Oh, the look on Scudd's face when Mike grabbed him by the collar and yanked him back," Alisa reflected when she had regained enough control to speak again.

"Do you know. . ." Delilah suppressed a fresh burst of giggles. "I was thinking he should carry a handkerchief if he had a cold? I didn't realize. . ."

"He was sniffing you like a fresh-baked pie?" Miriam filled in.

"Served him right Mike reined him in," Reba observed tartly. "Those MacPhersons sure are an interesting bunch, but they've got their hearts in the right place. Now." She straightened up. "We've got a passel of hungry men out there, so we'd best get stuff on the tables."

ᔕ

Paul glowered impartially at the horde of men around the barn as they gathered to try their hand at horseshoes.

"I'm of a mind to think that the real winner today may not be the man who hooks the most shoes." Ross Dorsey grinned.

"Yep. It's the man who snags that purty little new filly on Chance Ranch," another man agreed.

"Just so's it ain't another one of you brothers," Rusty griped.

"She's not a brood mare, fellas." Bryce joined Paul in scowling.

"Easy enough fer you ta say with three women on your spread," someone scoffed. "You're the best-fed, best-dressed, luckiest men around."

"And you know it!" Nathan Bates chimed in.

"Not to mention the other benefits," someone grumbled.

Paul started toward the upstart, ready to begin a brawl. Broken arm or not, he wasn't going to listen to them talk that way about Delilah, Miriam, or Alisa. Daniel grabbed his good arm, bringing him to a stop almost before he'd started.

"I don't want to hear that kind of talk. These are good women—ladies." Daniel glowered at all and sundry of the neighbors, whose reaction reminded Paul just which brother was best at this sort of thing.

"Aw, we didn't mean nothin' by it, Danny-boy. We're right glad to have 'em livin' hereabouts."

"They's shore nice 'bout whippin' up a mess o' vittles fer us ev'ry week," Obie piped up.

"And it's nice just to be around 'em."

"Yeah, just enjoying their company, is all," Ross agreed.

"Hey, Scudd," someone exclaimed. "What'd she smell like?"

"Didya get a snootful?" another man eagerly asked.

"I shorely did." Scudd closed his eyes blissfully, then cracked one open to make sure he had a captive audience before continuing. "Smells jist as purty as the little gal looks. Like a flower in spring." Several men nodded and smiled.

Paul shrugged out of Daniel's grasp and stomped nearer. "Don't any of you be getting ideas."

To his surprise, Mike stepped over to his side, reminding Paul just who'd come to Delilah's rescue earlier when he'd been sitting too far away.

"Here I thought I'd learned ya about that. If'n ya need another lesson in manners, I'd be plum tickled ta oblige. Seems ta me you could use a good thumpin'."

Scudd bristled visibly. "It was worth it, and I'd do it again."

"You'd better not," Paul warned.

"Course not," Scudd agreed quickly, falling back a step.

Satisfied, Paul turned to face the rest of the town. "We've been through this enough times you all should know better. Any woman under our roof is as good as family—"

"I'll say, seein' as how they become family. You brothers are called Chance 'cuz ya don't give anyone else a chance to catch a bride," Rusty complained. "Ya hog 'em all."

"Yeah. Seems to me like we can figger who's got an eye on this one," Ross challenged. "You gonna stake yer claim?"

Paul found himself on the receiving end of several accusing glares but refused to back down. "She's not a piece of land, and well you know it. Listen, she just lost her pa, so you all need to back off."

"So long as you play by the same rules."

Paul pushed back a twinge of guilt at the pointed comment.

"She's Miriam's cousin," Gideon added, "so I'll take it personally if she's bothered."

"And that means she's kin to my daughters," Daniel reminded all and sundry.

"So don't give us reason to ask you to leave," Paul finished.

"That's enough," Gus broke in. "I'm too old to waste what time I've got left listenin' to y'all argue. Now, which one of you whippersnappers thinks he can take me on at horseshoes?"

&a

That night, Daniel helped Paul take off his boots.

"Still in a temper, eh?" Daniel broke the silence.

"Just thinking." Paul shrugged, not liking the direction his brother was headed. He'd only heard that tone of voice from Daniel when he was talking to Polly or Ginny Mae. "I don't like every last man in the township circling around her like vultures."

"Well, it seems to me maybe you're doing the wrong thinking. Being sweet on a woman isn't supposed to turn you sour."

Paul looked at his brother in silent disbelief.

"Don't you give me that look. I'm different. It wasn't loving Hannah that took it out of me. It was losing her. And I'm telling you right now, you can't lose what you never had, so you've no call to be looking like somebody put a hole in your favorite hat."

That coaxed a smile from Paul. "Here I thought you were mad about how Delilah threw that knife."

"You got that right. Still, I can't in good conscience send Delilah off to any of the rabble lurking around today. She's one of ours now. And if you aim to keep it that way, you'd best do a bit less thinking and a lot more courting."

"Don't you think I want to?" Paul ran his fingers through his hair in frustration. "I'm praying on it, but she isn't a believer, Dan. You know what the Bible says about being unequally yoked."

"What makes you think she doesn't believe?" Surprise colored Dan's words.

"We've spoken about it."

"I'm glad to see you haven't been sittin' on your hands this whole time, then. Let me tell you what I've learned, because I have something in common with little Miss Delilah. The Lord took loved ones from both of us. And as angry as I am with Him, and no matter how much I disagree with what He does, I still know He exists. I'm just not so sure He's worth trusting anymore. Delilah's the same way. She may not trust Him, but she believes He exists, whether she admits it or not."

Paul mulled that over for a minute. "So you really do believe in Him? You don't just tolerate it for Hannah's memory?"

"Look. This isn't about me. I'm just saying that Delilah's had a rough time of it, and you've got your work cut out for you. But if you're going to convince her to trust you and God, you can't look so surly. Besides," Daniel grumbled as he pulled up a blanket, "the sooner you manage it, the sooner I can get some peace and quiet."

৵

"Mornin'." Any lingering goodwill Paul had toward the MacPherson brothers for their actions two days ago vanished like—well, like a biscuit set in front of one of them! This made the third time they'd shown up in only four days, and Paul wasn't about to believe they'd lost track of the date this time around.

"Mornin'." He waited in silence, determined not to make this easy for them. They shifted in their saddles.

"Can we'uns have a word with Miz Delilah?" Hezzy failed to ease the tension. "We brung her summat."

Paul didn't like the sound of that. "Well, I'm sure she's busy right now, so how about I pass it along for you?"

Mike eyed him with a knowing glint. "I don' blame ya fer bein' less'n pleased ta clap eyes on us agin'—you bein' clever folks an' all. Still, I reckon we can be civil 'bout this. Ya know we don't mean no harm and won' try an' take no privliges like some."

"Ya know we jist come to give her those seeds fer her garden," Obie protested, obviously missing the new turn of conversation.

Paul didn't like the sound of that at all. The garden was his and Delilah's—a thing shared and fostered like their relationship. Unfortunately, Paul had to admit, Mike had the right of it. The MacPhersons didn't have the best manners, but they did have class where it counted.

"Why don't you come on in?" Paul invited and led them to the house, where they found the women making bacon sandwiches and fixing green beans.

"Hello." Miriam looked up from the table where she worked with Polly on the alphabet.

"Good morning." Delilah smiled and wiped her hands on her apron before ringing the dinner bell.

"We brung ya this." Hezzy thrust a sack toward her.

"Thank you, but I really don't think I can accept it," Delilah said softly.

"How come? Mike says it's proper fer a fella ta take a lady flowers." Obie's brow furrowed.

"Oh, well, thank you." Delilah hesitantly accepted the sack. "This doesn't feel like flowers."

"That's 'cuz they's better'n flowers. They's seeds from Meemaw's gardin back home." Hezzy beamed at her.

"I thunk on it when ya tol' us 'bout yer garden, Miz Delilah." Micah fiddled with his hat brim.

"That's so thoughtful." She smiled at all three of them. "But really, you should keep them so one day they'll brighten up your homes."

"Aw, no sense in that. We ain't got much skill fer growin' things. Someone ought to enjoy 'em. It'll do us good ta see sommat from Hawk's Fall, Miz Delilah."

"In that case, I'd be happy to grow some for you. When they bloom, you can take some home on Sundays," Delilah graciously accepted as the Chance brothers tromped in and started washing up.

"Something wrong?" Gideon went straight to Miriam's side and looked at the MacPhersons.

"No, honey. The MacPhersons were just being neighborly and brought Delilah some seeds for the garden." Miriam turned to their guests. "And of course they'll be staying for lunch."

That does it, Paul resolved as Mike wrangled a seat on Delilah's other side, *I'm making a second table*.

eleven

As before, the MacPhersons dug into the meal with gusto. It really was sweet of them to bring her those seeds, but Delilah decided not to use them all. That way, when the brothers had wives of their own, she could give them back. Delilah certainly had no plans to become one of those women, though.

"You're lookin' mighty fine today, Miz Delilah." Micah almost sounded as though he'd practiced the compliment.

"Thank you." Delilah focused on her green beans.

"Yep. A bit long in the too—" Hezzy broke off as Obie jabbed him in the side with his elbow.

"But we ain't seen a gal so purty since the Trevor sisters back home." Rather than being offended, Delilah choked back laughter with her beans. Surely no woman had ever been faced with such earnest suitors as she!

"What'd they look like?" Logan perked up visibly.

"Oh, hair like a log afire," Obie reminisced.

"Eyes jist as shiny as a mud puddle," Hezzy added. "Nary one single gap from a tooth a-missin'."

Delilah fought to keep a straight face at this high praise for the Trevor sisters. And to think, she had the honor of being the next prettiest woman they'd ever seen!

"Sweetest li'l thangs ya could ever hope ta see. Only saw 'em onc't, though."

"Are they nice?" Ginny Mae asked, obviously concerned with issues more important than physical beauty.

"O'course, li'l missy. Their uncle raised coon dogs. That's

how we met 'em, gettin' ole Bear. Right fine animal—worth the trip down ta the holler, let me tell you." Obie was clearly lost in his memories.

"If they have a way with animals, there's somethin' good inside them." Bryce nodded his approval.

"Shore as shootin'," Hezzy agreed. "Critters always know. Course, some critters are best in a pot."

"They made a fine mess o' squirrel stew. Made the meat so nice it almost tasted like possum." Obie took a swig of water.

"How come you didn't marry them?" Polly asked with a bluntness only a child could display.

"Aw, didn't have nothin' ta offer two fine wimmen like them," Hezzy explained. "That's why we'uns come here—ta make somethin' o' ourselves."

"And we done it." Mike leaned back and crossed his arms over his chest. "Now we gots us a spread o' good land and cattle."

"How many Trevor sisters are there?" Paul asked Mike.

"Cain't say. I ain't never seen 'em," Mike scoffed.

"Two," Obie supplied.

"Anybody you liked better?" Daniel shot Paul a conspiratorial glance.

"Aw, I don' know."

Delilah was surprised to see the tips of Mike's ears turn red.

"Come on, we're all friends here," Miriam encouraged.

"Well, I suppose I've gotta soft spot for Miss Temperance. Her sister was the healer, and she'd come ta help Ma. Tempy would cook for us or sing to Ma ta pass the time. Smart, too. Got a good head on her shoulders."

"You've done well for yourselves," Paul joined in. "Why don't you write to them?"

"Mike's the only one as cain write any," Obie pointed out.

" 'Sides," Hezzy joined in, "they cain't read anywho."

"Tempy can," Mike said softly. " 'Sides, askin' a woman to travel away from her kin has ta be done proper-like. I cain't do that good."

His simple answer tugged at Delilah's heart. Mike obviously held Tempy in high esteem. These were good men, and they deserved good women. *Maybe I can help.*

"How about if I helped you write the letter? You just tell me what you want said."

"Hey, what about our'n?" Obie jabbed a thumb to indicate Hezzy.

"Well. . ." Delilah thought a moment.

"Couldn't we send it to Tempy and ask her to pass along the message?" Paul suggested.

"I reckon that jist might work." After a long silence in which both brothers thought so hard they looked strained, Obie agreed. "Mike?"

"It bears thinkin' on." Mike didn't say yes but seemed to be giving the idea serious consideration. "Are the both of ya set on those gals?"

"As the sun goes down of a mornin'," came Hezzy's solemn vow.

"The sun comes up in the mornin', but I ken whatcha mean," Mike allowed. "Which one do ya each fancy?"

Obie and Hezzy stared at each other for a long minute. "Don't recollect their names, Mike."

"Eunice and Lois," Hezzy said.

"Oh, yeah. Tha' sounds 'bout right. Ya got a pref'rence, Hezzy?" Obie generously inquired.

"Not sure I could tell the two apart, come ta thunk on it." Hezzy looked at Delilah. "That gonna be a problem?"

"Um. . ." She seriously wondered whether or not this would work. "I suppose if we worded it right, we could just say you two remember them fondly and would be honored if they'd come and join you in the hopes of matrimony."

"That do sound purty as a poem. D'ya reckon it'd work?" Hezzy beseeched Mike.

"No harm in tryin'." Mike sighed.

"Well, why don't you all think about what you'd like to say. If they're coming, we need to send for them soon enough so they can arrive before winter. Try to make it as personal as you can, and we'll write it up after you've had a chance to think on it."

"And pray!" Ginny Mae piped up. "Auntie Miri-Em always says to think and pray."

"All right. We'll see you later."

Delilah couldn't help but notice the air of excitement surrounding the MacPhersons as they took their leave. In hopes of avoiding their courting, she'd promised to do her best to snag them other women. *What have I gotten myself into?*

≈

"Hang on, we're comin'!" Paul buttoned his shirt and beat Daniel to the door, which he swung open. Miriam faced him, shifting her weight from foot to foot.

"What's wrong?" Panic surged through Paul's veins. Miriam wouldn't bother them in the morning unless it was something important.

"Today's Delilah's birthday! I forgot until last night when I was writing in my diary, and I saw that I'd marked the date."

Relief washed over him, only to be followed by an unsettled feeling as his stomach clenched. He had nothing to give the woman he hoped to wed. Even the MacPhersons had managed to give her something!

"Exactly." Miriam nodded her approval at his reaction. "So here's what we're going to do. . . ."

❧

"Can we have carrot sticks on our picnic, Auntie Lilah?" Ginny Mae tugged on her skirts. "I likes carrot sticks."

Delilah smiled as she wrapped the carrots in a cloth and placed them in a basket. Miriam was so thoughtful to suggest a picnic lunch today. She and Paul would take the girls out for fun and perhaps even a sketching lesson for Polly. Delilah might sketch something worth turning into a painting.

"All right. Have you got Dolly?" Ginny Mae ran to the table, grabbed her dolly off the bench, and clutched it to her chest.

"Uh-huh. And Aunt Miri-Em gots an old blankie." The toddler gave a short hop of excitement. "Can we goes now?"

Delilah held Ginny Mae's hand and grabbed the basket. "Let's go!"

Outside, Paul stood by the wagon where Polly nestled atop the folded old quilt. "Ready?"

Paul helped Delilah and Ginny Mae scramble into the back of the wagon, then took the seat. He'd reassured them he could handle one horse for a short ride without any problems.

He was as good as his word, pulling up under a stand of trees with just enough leaves to offer some shade. They spread out the blanket as Paul tied the horse's reins loosely around a tree.

The girls ran and twirled around for a while.

"It's a lovely day," he commented. "We've got everything we need. Good company, sunshine, shade, and a nice view." His gaze rested on Delilah.

"And clouds! I like clouds!" Polly pointed at the sky.

"That one," Delilah joined in, "could be a little castle, like in fairy tales. See the tower?"

"Oooh," Polly breathed. "I wish our house looked like that!"

"Hmmm. . ." Paul stroked his chin. "That one's white,

fluffy, round. . . . I'd say it looks like a biscuit to me!"

"Yummy!" Ginny Mae clapped.

"Can we have some now?" Polly pleaded.

"Well, I don't see why not. What've you got in that basket, Delilah?"

"Carrot sticks." Ginny Mae imparted her wisdom, presenting her treasure with a flourish.

Delilah smiled as the little girl began passing out the carrot sticks. She pulled out a canteen of iced tea, some cold chicken, a wedge of cheese, and some of those renowned biscuits.

She and Paul helped Polly and Ginny Mae make sandwiches, and they all munched happily. After lunch, Delilah pulled out her sketchbook and pencil.

"What're you doing?" Polly scooted over to take a look.

"Drawing that hill over there with the trees."

Polly watched in fascination as the lines became tree trunks and grass. "Why are you only coloring in part of it?"

"It's called shading. It's to show where the light was, so when I paint over it, I get the colors right."

"That's pretty." Polly stood up and walked over to a tree with lots of branches. Reaching up, she grabbed a branch and stuck her foot into a knothole, hoisting herself onto the lowest level. "See? I like trees!" She stretched for the next branch.

"No higher, Polly," Paul admonished.

Privately, Delilah thought even that low branch, close to the ground as it rested, was already too high.

With a gamine grin, Polly scrambled up, only to shriek as Paul grabbed her with his good arm and swung her down.

"That was fun!" She giggled.

"Was it worth disobeying?"

Her smile faded at Paul's tone. "Sorry, Uncle Paul." She buried her face in his shoulder.

"You know better. Now you won't get to share some of that apple pie I saw in our picnic basket."

Her head jerked up and her lower lip quivered. "But I like apple pie." She wailed.

"You'll remember to listen to your elders next time, though. Now, go on and play with Ginny Mae." Paul set her down and patted her on the back.

Polly threw one last yearning look at the picnic basket, then trundled off to chase a butterfly with Ginny Mae.

He'll be a wonderful father. Gentle with the girls, but firm in discipline.

He plunked down next to Delilah and tugged the sketchbook out of her hands. He studied the drawing, then the landscape, then held the sketchbook up and squinted. Delilah's heart thumped as she waited for his opinion.

≈

Paul studied the sketch in silence. *How can black and white seem so lifelike? Why does everything she touches gain beauty?*

"If this one weren't in black and white, it'd be just like looking out a window. It's that true to the land. God's given you quite a gift, Delilah."

Her cheeks grew rosy at his praise. "I don't know about that. I draw and paint because I remember Mama teaching me how. When it comes down to it, though, I didn't make the trees or the sky. I enjoy their beauty enough to copy them. This is just an imitation." She tapped the sketch.

"It's wonderful, and I think God will look upon it as a compliment." Paul meant every word. *It was a shame she didn't see it that way yet because her art was an eloquent form of praise.*

"Do you have to bring God into everything?" Disappointment clouded her amber eyes.

How do I answer her, Lord? Please give me the words.

"I don't bring Him into anything, Delilah. His hand created all you see before you. All that is beautiful comes from Him."

She was silent for a while; the only sounds were the girls' giggles as they rolled down one of the smaller hills.

"Maybe." Delilah stood up. "We ought to be getting back. Polly! Ginny Mae! Come on back!" Keeping her back to him, she gathered and folded the quilt, placing it and the basket in the buckboard.

Lord, will she ever accept You? Or me?

twelve

Paul's the best man I've ever met—and we're too different to be together. He bases his entire life on something he can't see or touch. Delilah's frustrated thoughts bounced around as much as the buckboard did on the bumpy road they took to return to the ranch.

She put her arm around Polly and snuggled the five-year-old to her side. Ginny Mae crawled into Delilah's lap and fought to keep her eyes open as the wagon swayed over the path. How could anyone not see how precious children and security were? Delilah, for one, intended to make them her priority for every minute she spent at Chance Ranch.

They pulled up to the barn, and Paul helped her out of the wagon. Delilah cuddled Ginny Mae in the bed of the buckboard as Paul took care of the horse, then scooped Polly into his arm. It seemed as though he wanted to say something, but he turned away.

She stopped him, only to find herself unsure of what to say. She couldn't let their day together end this way.

"I enjoyed our picnic." It sounded feeble to her ears, but Paul accepted the gesture.

"Someday you'll see that we're not as different as you think." His tender smile lifted her spirits. "Come on, they'll be waiting on us for supper."

Together they walked to the house, where Miriam and Alisa were just setting an enormous pork roast on the table.

"If I'd known you were going to prepare a feast today,"

Delilah said, eying the mashed potatoes, peas, and corn bread, "I would've helped instead of going on the picnic."

"Balderdash." Alisa sat down. "You know very well you helped with breakfast and looked after the girls today."

They all joined hands as Titus blessed the meal and thanked the Lord. Everyone stayed strangely silent, but then again, the food tasted so wonderful, no one seemed too concerned with conversation. Even Polly, having missed her afternoon nap, yawned instead of chattering like a magpie. When everyone had eaten their fill, Delilah rose and began to help Miriam clear the table.

"Oh, Delilah." Alisa stopped her. "There's something the men wanted to show you. Since we've already seen it, Miriam and I will take care of the dishes." She winked at Titus, who gallantly offered Delilah his arm.

Intrigued, Delilah accepted, following Daniel and Gideon to her cabin.

"Now, close your eyes," Daniel ordered.

Feeling slightly apprehensive, Delilah obeyed. She heard the door creak softly as Titus led her forward.

"All right. Open 'em." The words barely left Gideon's lips before Delilah gasped.

They'd whitewashed the cabin while she'd been gone!

"It's wonderful," she breathed, crossing the room and turning around to take it all in. The cabin gleamed, somehow larger and brighter. "Thank you so much!"

Gideon and Titus grinned while Daniel shrugged. "Didn't take long with the three of us."

"We used the whitewash left over from what Miriam bought," Gideon explained.

"Alisa thought you might like it." Titus smiled fondly at the mere mention of his wife.

"I love it." Delilah fought back tears at the thoughtful gesture. "Thank you so much." She saw that they'd done their level best to make this cabin her home.

But it's not my home. It's Paul's.

"Will Paul mind?" she asked, hesitant to make it seem as though she didn't appreciate the surprise, but anxious to hear the answer.

Titus laughed. "Why do you think he took you and the girls on the picnic?"

Happiness blossomed. Paul knew—he'd spent a lovely day with her so she could be surprised when they got back. He's such a generous man.

"Miriam and Alisa'll want to know what you think." Gideon nudged her toward the door. Still not quite believing it, she cast one last look over her shoulder, then rushed back to the kitchen to envelop Alisa and Miriam in a hug. "Thank you! It's so lovely—I can hardly believe you did it just for me!"

Alisa laughed. "We thought you might like it."

"It's astounding what a little whitewash can do for a room." Miriam voiced exactly what Delilah thought. "Now, it's time to blow out your candles!"

For the first time, Delilah noticed the large cake on the table.

"Happy birthday!" everyone chorused as she took a huge breath and blew out all of the candles.

"Wait a minute!" Logan stopped Miriam as she began cutting the cake. "Bryce and I have something for Delilah, too."

Bryce carried in a crate lined with scraps from an old quilt. He set it down on the bench. Curious, Delilah leaned over to see a small, white and brown ball of fur.

Bryce gently picked it up, and Delilah recognized a kitten just big enough to fit in the palm of his hand. "This here's

Shortstack. Normally we keep the cats in the barn, but her mama had a big litter and Shortstack—" Bryce set her on the table to demonstrate "—has one leg that's a bit shorter than the other three." The little cat started ambling toward the cake. "She can get by but just can't keep up with the rest and might not be able to move fast enough around the cows and horses."

Logan scooped her up and placed the tiny kitten in Delilah's hands. "We thought maybe you'd like to keep her."

Delilah lifted the cat up for a closer view. She gently stroked the soft fur. "Oh, she's adorable!" Delilah lost her heart when the kitten curled up in her cupped hands. "I think she and I will get along just fine."

Logan positively beamed. "You can keep the crate in your cabin—it's where she'll sleep. She's big enough now she doesn't need her mama. She'll do with a saucer of milk."

Feeling as though her heart would burst, Delilah placed her new friend back in the nest of scraps. She'd never experienced such a wonderful birthday. This entire family had given their whole day to making her feel special, and she knew she'd never forget it. Daniel put the girls to bed while everyone else relaxed.

"Well, you certainly had a busy day!" Delilah exclaimed when Alisa held up the forest green day dress with an extra length of black added to the hem and sleeves so it would fit Delilah perfectly.

"Oh, it was nothing," Alisa demurred and pushed a small package toward her. "Open Miriam's!"

Delilah tugged the string and brown paper off to reveal the small teakwood treasure box she'd admired earlier.

"But this is one of the few things from your home, Miriam!" Delilah protested. "You should keep it."

"My home is here now, and so is yours. You should have a few special things in your cabin." Miriam always knew just what to say to put her at ease.

Delilah looked at Paul. "Thank you for letting them white-wash the cabin. I hope you like it, too, so it won't bother you when I leave."

His brow furrowed. "What do you mean, when you leave? That's your cabin now."

"Yeah! We can always build another one." Logan's frown matched his older brother's.

Sorry to have ruined everyone's good time, Delilah tried to backtrack. "Oh, I'm sure you can. But I can't stay here forever. Things will change sooner or later, you know. But I do love it here."

Paul smiled again. "Good, because this week I'll teach you to drive a buckboard. I know it's not exactly a present—"

"Every day here is something I enjoy," Delilah interjected. "And you know I want to learn, so you'll be giving me a new skill. I look forward to it."

Daniel returned, and Gideon began an evening devotional before they all turned in for the night. Delilah brought her new pet into her cabin.

"You'll sleep right here where I can see you." Delilah crossed her arms after pushing the crate right next to her bed.

Shortstack opened her tiny mouth in a feline yawn and kneaded the blanket as she settled in. Delilah smiled and hopped into bed. Tomorrow she planned on painting that sketch she'd drawn today. It couldn't be a grand gesture, but she wanted to give something back to these warm-hearted people who'd given her so much.

❧

"Well, at least you don't spoil her," Paul teased Delilah as she set down a saucer of cream on the stoop for Shortstack's breakfast.

"That's what Bryce told me to give her." Delilah grabbed the watering can while the kitten daintily lapped her breakfast.

"Calm down. I think she likes you, too." He watched as Shortstack finished her breakfast and brushed up against Delilah's skirts, trying to twine around her ankles.

"I never knew I could become so fond of something so fast." She smiled as the kitten gave a slightly unsteady hop off the threshold.

Paul waited until Delilah looked at him again to reply. He met her gaze. "I know exactly what you mean." He saw his remark sunk home when she blushed and turned her attention to the watering can, practically flooding a tiny sprout before regaining her composure and moving on.

I can't wait until I give her our first driving lesson.

❧

Later that morning, Paul finished inspecting all the tack and tending to the leather, then went to find Delilah. Garbed in some sort of stained smock, she stood in a patch of sunlight beside the barn, the tip of her tongue between her lips as she concentrated. A speck of green paint dotted her nose while some stray curls escaped her loose bun to wave in the slight breeze. Paul had never seen a woman look more beautiful.

He just stood there, watching, hesitant to startle her for fear it would ruin her work. Shortstack gave him away, ambling toward him and attracting Delilah's attention with a mewling cry.

Self-consciously, she lifted a hand to smooth her hair, only to stop when she saw her colorful fingertips.

"Hi," Paul said softly.

"Hi." She waved her brush toward the picture. "If you wait

for a minute, you can be the first to see it."

More than happy she hadn't sent him away, Paul plunked down to play with Shortstack while she finished.

A few moments later, she stepped back with a satisfied sigh. "I'm done."

Paul got to his feet and strode to where she stood, very aware of her anxious gaze upon his face as he scrutinized the piece.

What he saw almost rivaled its creator in loveliness. "Amazing. It's as though I'm sitting with you on that very same hill!"

A smile spread across her face. "Good. That's just what I wanted—something so the Chance family would remember yesterday for as long as I will." She looked away shyly and confessed, "I'm hoping everyone will want to hang it in the parlor."

"You've got my vote. It's plain to see how talented you are."

"Well, it's about time I wash up and go help with lunch." She picked up the watercolor and headed toward her cabin. Paul noticed her slower pace as Shortstack gamboled along beside her.

Paul stifled a groan when he spotted the all-too-familiar cloud of dust on the horizon just before lunch. This time, instead of trying to dissuade the stubborn clan from coming in, he'd just go inside and let the women know who was coming

At least this visit from the MacPhersons had one thing in its favor—they wouldn't be trying to woo his woman but rather be soliciting her expert assistance in courting other brides. Come to think of it, the sooner they wrote those letters, the quicker they wouldn't have any reason to barge onto Chance Ranch whenever the mood struck them.

Paul's good humor lasted through lunch and right up until Delilah and the MacPhersons huddled at the table—alone.

❧

"All right, what do you have for me so far?" Delilah eyed the trio of brothers with some misgivings.

Micah reached into his shirt pocket and drew out some grubby paper. He smoothed it on the table and wordlessly slid it toward her.

Delilah looked in consternation at the few words penned across the sheet.

"But, these are just their names and where to send it."

Micah jabbed it with a finger. "Naw, it ain't. That there's the name of their aunt."

Obie nodded eagerly. "Figgered we oughta pass along our respects an' all."

"That's a wonderful idea. It can't hurt to be on good terms with their family." Delilah desperately tried to think of a way to coax more information out of the would-be swains without discouraging them.

"They's sweet li'l thangs. We done tole Mike to write that down." Obie peered at the paper as though he'd suddenly be able to read.

"Oh, yes. I see it here, along with 'nice-sounding voices.' Um, I believe I heard you mention something about how they look?" she prodded.

"Yep. Hair redder'n a rooster's comb," Hezzy complimented.

Red hair, Delilah made a note, omitting the comparison to a rooster. "And you said something about their eyes. . . ."

Obie and Hezzy stared fixedly at the tabletop, so Delilah took a deep breath and pressed on. "I seem to remember you said they were shiny?"

Obie brightened and jabbed a thumb toward Hezzy. "Yep. He said as how they's jist as shiny as a mud puddle."

Delilah bit back a laugh at the extravagant praise. "Hmmm. . .

might I suggest something a bit more romantic?"

Hezzy frowned in concentration, then broke into a self-satisfied grin. "Sure. How 'bout eyes jist as shiny as a mud puddle. . . ." He paused to slant a triumphant look at Mike. "In the moonlight."

"Why, Hezzy, that's almost like po'try!" Obie slapped his brother's shoulder.

"Some things just don't sound the same on paper." Delilah diplomatically rejected the entire mud-puddle comparison. "How about 'browner than. . .'" She paused to think, belatedly realizing her mistake when they began offering suggestions.

"Dirt?" Obie supplied.

"Aw, ya don' say she's like dirt." Hezzy spared Delilah having to reject that pearl. "How 'bout bark?"

Her relief faded like a curtain left too long in the sun. "You know, there are different kinds of bark, so maybe you want to be more specific."

"A chaw a tobaccy?"

"A tater?" Soon the suggestions were flying through the air so fast, Delilah didn't even have to comment.

"Boot leather?"

"Molasses?"

"Fresh coffee?"

"Oh, that's a good un, Obie," Hezzy approved. "But ladies don' always like coffee like we uns. How 'bout 'the wings of a June bug'?"

With dismay, Delilah realized all three thought this analogy had merit. "Well, I don't know. I don't much like insects, myself."

Mike spoke up for the first time. "How 'bout brown as a fawn's coat?"

"Wonderful," Delilah praised, writing it down and moving

on before they could suggest anything else. "And I understand you wrote something to Temperance, Mike?"

"All done with that."

"So, they're sweet, with nice voices, red hair, brown eyes, and an aunt we'll need to win over. Is there anything else I'm missing?" She clearly needed to end this session before they backed her into a corner with their woeful wooing.

Hezzy spoke up. "They cook a right fine meal."

"And they's good gals. Not loose or. . .or anythin'." Obie wouldn't meet Delilah's eyes.

"God fearin' folk," Hezzy affirmed.

"And I've already explained to Tempy about our spread and what's waitin fer 'em," Mike assured her.

"Well, gentleman, I'll write this up and show you a draft next Sunday." She rose from the table, and the brothers followed suit.

"Much obliged," Mike thanked her.

As the brothers made their way out of the cabin, Delilah paused to wonder whether any man would ever write her a romantic letter.

thirteen

As most of the town headed back home after church that Sunday, the MacPhersons and Whites lingered at Chance Ranch.

Delilah looked at the three expectant faces before her, and the enormity of the situation sank in like never before. So much hinged on her writing—the dreams of Obie and Hezzy, the futures of Eunice and Lois—her throat went dry. Obie hunkered down to rub Shortstack's tummy as the kitten purred happily.

"I tried to mention everything you shared with me," she began, "so I'll just read it to you, and we'll see if you'd like to change any of it:

Dear Miss Eunice and Lois Trevor,

I, Delilah Chadwick, am writing this letter on behalf of my neighbors, Obadiah and Hezekiah MacPherson, who pray you are well. These upstanding brothers hold you in high regard and speak fondly of you both.

They describe your hair as rivaling a blazing sunset and admire your eyes as being as soft and brown as a fawn's spring coat. They tell me you are good, God-fearing women who will come alongside their men to make a home for their families.

They hope you remember the time they visited your home to purchase their hunting dog and ask you to pass along their compliments to your aunt and uncle for raising two such fine young women.

If you are agreeable and not already spoken for, the Misters MacPherson will send fare for your journey to their spread as their intended brides.

We send this in the care of Miss Temperance Spencer, whose hand Micah MacPherson has requested. They earnestly hope she will be your companion as you travel to Reliable, California.

Sincerely Yours,
Obie and Hezzy MacPherson

"Whooeee, if that don't turn they heads, sure as shootin' nothin' will." Hezzy clapped Obie on the shoulder. "We's gonna have us some brides, Brother!"

"Yep. That sounded so fine, I reckon if'n I got it, I'd marry us." Obie beamed at Delilah.

"How soon can we send it?" Mike got straight down to business.

"Oh, I'll take it back to town with me this evening, seal it, and send it out with the next batch of post." Reba White walked over. "So you boys are fixin' to get hitched, eh?"

"Yes'm," Obie and Hezzy chorused.

"All right. I'll let you know just as soon as they write back." Reba took the envelope from Delilah as they all exchanged good-byes.

"So we'll be seeing you on Thursday?" Delilah asked, knowing Miriam had invited the older woman over for a girls' sewing day.

"It's amazing how mending can pile up." Reba laughed ruefully. "And I've even got a quilt that's only half-finished. It'll do me good to spend a day in the company of women."

❧

"All right, now this is just a first lesson, so no need to be nervous." Finally, they were alone. Paul caught Delilah glancing from the reins to the horse and back again.

"Just the same, maybe we oughta wait until your arm is a bit better—in case. . ." Her voice faded as she looked at him pleadingly.

"Any woman who can wield a knife and shoot like you can has no need to fear driving," he consoled. "Besides, you already know how to handle a horse when you ride."

"That's because I can get the feel of the animal. I can touch him or use my voice to calm him down if he gets excited or frightened. I know enough about how an animal that doesn't know you won't trust you. They sense when the person guiding them is hesitant or doubtful."

"Speck is my horse. I trained him up from a colt—that's why he pulls the wagon, too. We understand each other, so he won't give us any trouble."

Delilah eyed the sling on Paul's arm with obvious misgivings but held her tongue.

Appreciating her tact, Paul decided to try it her way. "Would you feel better if you gave old Speck here some carrots and patted him a bit before we go? That way you could get to know him."

"Yes, I think that just might work." Relief colored her voice, and a smile returned to her lips.

"Do you feel comfortable holding his reins while I go grab some of those carrots?" She nodded, and he went to fetch some sugar cubes and carrots.

Lord, if I can say one thing about this woman You've brought into my life, it's that she's consistent. She doesn't trust Thee, and until she does, she can't trust me, and Speck doesn't stand a chance. I wonder whether she even trusts herself. Please be with us today so she'll feel the peace of Thy presence and gain no further reason to withdraw from others.

"You're a handsome fella." Paul squelched a spurt of envy when he realized Delilah was crooning to Speck. She stroked his mane and grinned at Paul when he stepped next to her.

"He's a beautiful animal, Paul. Sweet, too." She took the chunks of carrot and held them out to Speck, giggling when he lipped them from her hand.

"Kind of tickles, doesn't it?" Paul commiserated as Speck chomped his treat and buried his nose in her hands searching for more.

"Now, don't be greedy," Delilah chided. "We're going for a little ride, and afterwards you can have some more. Ready?"

Paul helped her into the buckboard, then jumped in beside her. "Now, to get Speck going, you give the reins a bit of a flick and give him the command." To illustrate, he clacked his tongue, and the wagon gave a slight lurch as Speck obeyed. "I want you to hold the reins with both hands." He waited until she had them securely in her hands before letting go.

"And I just hold them?"

"Make sure you don't let the line go slack, or he can have his head and yank the reins out of your hand. Then we have a runaway wagon."

She blanched, and he hastened to reassure her. "Just keep a good grip on them." Her knuckles went white as she clutched onto the leather. "How's this?"

"If you keep on like that, you'll cramp up. Relax a little. Pulling the reins will make him slow down. If you say, 'Whoa, boy,' and tug on them, he'll stop."

"Good. Whoa, boy," Delilah called, tightening the reins. A relieved smile crossed her face as the buckboard came to a halt. "That wasn't so bad."

"Very good," Paul praised. "But if you're going faster, remember you'll need to slow down before telling him to stop, or it'll be too sudden."

"Makes sense." Delilah, obviously feeling more in control, flicked the reins and clacked her tongue, grinning as Speck began to walk forward once again. "I think I've got the hang of it."

"You've got starting and stopping down, but there's a lot more to it," he warned, not wanting her to get too complacent.

"I suppose. How do I get him to move a little faster?"

"If you want him to speed it up, you flick the reins again and tell him to giddyup. Go ahead and try it. Remember that if you want him to slow down, just tug on the reins—but don't yank."

Soon she had Speck going at a jaunty trot. "Do you think I should try an even quicker pace?"

"If you ever actually want to get to town, you'll have to step it up a bit. Go ahead and have him go into a slow run—a canter."

"Oh, that's a big difference." Delilah gasped and tugged the reins, breathing more easily when the horse dropped back into a clip. "You did a wonderful job training him. He does exactly what I ask."

Paul refused to puff up like a rooster at the compliment. "Animals are a lot like people. It takes time to earn their trust, but when you do, it's always worth the wait."

She stayed silent for a moment, then asked in a small voice, "Always?"

"Always," he repeated firmly. "Some take more time than others, but those are the ones who are most worth the effort." This time, she didn't respond at all.

He reached over and took the reins from her. "We'd best be getting back. Reba'll be here soon."

ta

Lost in thought, Delilah washed her hands slowly. Paul hadn't just been talking about horses.

He wants me to trust him, and I already trust him more than any man I've ever known—even Papa. As much as I loved him, he couldn't keep promises he made to himself, much less the ones he gave me. Paul has never broken his word to me or anyone else as far as I've seen. But that'll just make it so much harder when he finally does. No one's perfect, so how can I trust him more than I already do?

As she dried her hands, she wiped away the unsettling thoughts, then went to the parlor, where Reba, Alisa, and Miriam waited. Davie had a cold, so Widow Greene couldn't make it, and it was simply understood that Priscilla couldn't be bothered to stitch hems.

"I brought by some flannel for you, Miriam. Thought after we took care of the mending, we could make a few things for your firstborn son."

"So you think the baby will be a boy, too?" Alisa asked, slanting Delilah a victorious look.

"Be mighty surprised if we didn't have another Chance man on the ranch soon, seein' as how his papa has five brothers," Reba confirmed.

"But Miriam's side of the family runs to girls," Delilah protested. "Think about it—there's me, Miriam, and Hannah, and we're cousins because Grandma had two daughters in the first place. Then there's Polly and Ginny Mae, and Daniel has five Chance brothers, too. I'm not saying the babe won't be a boy; I just figure it could go either way."

"I suppose it could, come to that," Reba allowed.

"If you're all finished speculating, I can tell you." Miriam spoke softly, her hand resting on her rounded tummy. "My son will be born in early summer."

"Well, that settles it," Reba finished.

"Have you told Gideon?" Alisa asked.

"We've decided we'll name him Caleb after his grandpa." Miriam looked so content and proud, sitting there in the rocker Gideon had made for her and their babe, Delilah just had to get up and give her a hug. It didn't surprise her when Alisa joined them, and Reba came over to say a prayer.

"Lord, we thank Thee for Thy many blessings and lift up Miriam and her babe, Caleb, to Thy arms for protection and comfort."

Even Delilah couldn't help joining the fervent chorus of "Amens." If it might help Miriam and her child, she'd pray to their God.

"Why are you all smothering my wife?" Gideon demanded from the doorway.

Everyone untangled as Reba let loose a bark of laughter. "We were just having a woman moment, Gideon."

"Reba prayed for me and the babe." Miriam stood up and walked over to her husband, who put his arm around her and dropped a kiss on the top of her head.

"What are you doing here so early, honey?" she asked. "Supper's hours off yet."

"I knew you were all having a sewing day, so I figured I'd change and hand this over." He held out the brown chambray shirt he'd been wearing earlier that day. "Got caught in some thorny fence."

"Good thinking." Reba bobbed her head. "Nothin' worse than spending a day mending, only to have your man come home with another load."

"I'll just leave you women to it." Gideon left the room, and Alisa giggled.

"What's so funny?" Miriam asked.

"Nothing much. I couldn't help thinking your husband

might've felt a bit uncomfortable in here. It's not often the women outnumber the men on Chance Ranch."

Delilah couldn't hold back a chuckle at that observation. "Oh, I don't know. When Paul took me and the girls on a picnic for my birthday, he held his own."

"We all had a nice day." Alisa smiled at the memory. "Gideon, Daniel, and Titus finished whitewashing your cabin in no time at all. Logan and Bryce gave Shortstack a bath, if you'd believe it. Never would've thought dunking a feline would prove a challenge for two young men, but that cat was bound and determined not to get wet. Course in the end, Bryce and Logan had their way."

"I don't know about that." Miriam smiled as she threaded a needle. "I thought Shortstack matched 'em drop for drop when they came in looking like they'd been dunked in the fishing hole."

"And all my favorite food lay spread out like a feast when we got home. You two kept yourselves just as busy as the men." Delilah wanted to let them know how much she appreciated their kindness.

"Well, you did right by 'em in return." Reba nodded at the landscape hanging on the parlor wall. "Right before you came in, Miriam and Alisa were telling me how you painted that in thanks."

"Oh, that hardly took any time at all," Delilah assured her. "I sketched it that day while we were on the picnic and filled it in with watercolors the next day. I love painting."

"And it shows in every stroke," Miriam complimented.

"You've got a talent, that's for sure. That's a piece of art any rich man in the city would be proud to hang on his wall. Something peaceful and happy about it." Reba stared at the painting, her fingers darning a sock almost by memory.

"I wouldn't suppose you'd paint another one?" she wondered aloud.

"I don't paint anything in the exact same way twice," Delilah apologized.

"Oh, no. I didn't mean the same picture. I just mean another painting. It'd be a real nice addition to the store. I'd hang it right over the counter." The dreamy look on Reba's face faded as she took on the visage of a businesswoman once again. "I'd give you a fair deal in store credit."

"Oh, you're so nice to us. You'll be here for Miriam's birthing, too. I'd be happy to make you one as a gift, Reba."

"Nonsense. I wouldn't feel right about it." Reba looked across at her with a stern expression. "Now, you just have it for me some Sunday, and we'll set you up with that store credit. Do we have an understanding?"

"Agreed." Delilah couldn't find it in her heart to argue with the determined woman. "What type of landscape would you like?"

"Whaddya mean?"

"Well, I can paint the barn, or a grove of trees, or the creek," Delilah elaborated.

"Oh, you should paint the fishing hole!" Alisa encouraged.

"I think I'd like something with a bit of water in it," Reba mused. "Well, I trust you. Just go ahead and surprise me."

fourteen

"Delilah," Paul started to say as Polly and Ginny Mae peered down from the wagon. *How can I tell her that even though she's learning very quickly, I'd rather drive today? She's only had three lessons, and I don't want to risk Polly and Ginny Mae.*

While he searched for words, Delilah spoke. "If you don't mind, I think you should drive this afternoon. You're a wonderful teacher, but. . ." She smiled at the girls. "Today we carry precious cargo."

Lord, we are alike in so many ways. Why can't she see it? She values home and family, everything I want to give her. Please help me find the words to reach beyond the wall to her heart.

"We certainly do." He helped Delilah up into the back of the wagon and watched as Polly and Ginny Mae immediately scooted toward her. She wrapped an arm around each of them and listened attentively as Ginny Mae rattled off the beginning of the alphabet.

She'll be a wonderful mother. He let those pleasant thoughts run through his mind until they neared the fishing hole.

"I don't see any water." Delilah gave a slight frown and craned her neck to get a better view. "Is it past that hill?"

"Yep. Just past those trees and bushes." He gestured toward the greenery. Spring always touched the pond first. "It's best to leave the wagon right here and walk Speck up so he can have a drink."

Delilah lent a hand in unhitching the horse and held Speck's reins while Paul hefted down the girls and supplies.

He accepted the reins and led the way up the well-worn path. Glancing back, he saw Delilah holding the basket on one arm, with Ginny Mae clutching her hand and Polly's in her chubby fists, completing the chain. He hastily tied Speck to a tree and met them at the bushes.

"Before we get any closer, I need you dumplin's to listen to the rules." He knelt to be at eye level with Polly and Ginny Mae. *"Neither of you can swim, so you'll have to steer clear of the fishing hole—it's far too deep. Do you understand?"* The little heads bobbed in unison. *"And you're not to run off where Delilah and I can't see you."* That way, the girls wouldn't venture toward the creek, which ran a little ways off. *"Got it?"*

"Yes, Uncle Paul," the girls chorused as he took the basket from Delilah.

"All right, then. Let's go!" He started back up the path, only to see two tiny blurs race ahead of him beyond the bushes.

"Hey!" The girls froze at his roar.

"What did I just say about running off?"

"Sorry, Uncle Paul." Polly scuffed the toe of her shoe in the dirt.

"We got 'cited."

"If you do that again," Delilah shook her finger, "we'll go back home." Her stern demeanor crumbled when Polly's lower lip trembled and tears welled up in Ginny Mae's eyes.

She knelt down and gathered them in her arms. "We love you both very much, and it's our job to make sure you're safe. I'd rather take you home than see either of you get hurt."

"That's why you have to follow the rules," Paul finished for her.

"We'll be good." Polly hugged her.

"Pwomise," Ginny Mae vowed solemnly after a particularly loud sniff.

"Mind that you do," Paul said.

Two seconds later, all traces of crying evaporated.

"It's so pretty!" Polly stared around, awed at the lush vista.

The trees lent cool shade to the newly green hills as rays of sunshine sparkled through the leaves. Wildflowers nestled in clumps of clover, leading to the tall rushes tickling the water's edge. The tiny rivulets feeding the pond gurgled softly, underscoring the chirps of birds lining their nests. A calm breeze chased wispy white clouds across the sky and ruffled the grass along the small hills. Dragonflies skimmed the rippling water, where plump trout eyed them hungrily. Paul couldn't imagine anything closer to paradise than being in this place with the people he loved.

"It's wonderful," Delilah breathed, seeming to drink in her surroundings.

"No, Ginny Mae!" Polly grabbed her younger sister's hand as Ginny Mae toddled after a bright orange butterfly. "We ain't s'posed to go by any of the water." She cast a yearning glance at the cool pond.

"Well, now, that's not exactly true." Paul winked at Delilah. "There's one place you can play in the water. See over there?" He strode over to where a bubbling stream of water sprayed over a small outcropping of rocks to form a shallow pool, rolled up his sleeve, and touched the sandy bottom. The cool water lapped halfway up his forearm, not even reaching his elbow, while the stones at the top of the hill would be too high for the girls to touch. Dappled sunlight warmed the water, so he knew the girls wouldn't catch cold.

Polly and Ginny Mae hovered eagerly by his shoulder, anxious to get closer but hesitant to break the rules. They were good little girls and deserved a treat.

"I said you couldn't go where Delilah and I couldn't see you, and you couldn't be near the fishing hole. But as long as you obey those rules, you can play here in your very own pond."

"Complete with a tiny waterfall. It's perfect." Delilah helped the girls strip off their shoes and stockings.

Beaming, Polly scurried to the edge first, only to have her smile fade. "Uncle Paul, what're those?" She poked the water with a pink fingertip.

"Hmmm? Oh, those are just tadpoles. They won't hurt you."

"Whatsa tab-ole?" Ginny Mae toddled over.

"They're just baby frogs," Paul explained, taking Polly's hand.

"They don't look like frogs." Doubt still shone in her eyes as Paul slowly, gently guided her hand toward the water.

"They will later," Delilah said, backing him up. "You know, some people call them pollywogs."

"Really?" Polly giggled as the tadpoles flicked around her fingers. "That tickles!"

"Pollywog!" Ginny Mae shrieked in glee, pointing at her sister. "Pollywog!" Together they waded in, the water brushing just below Polly's knees and just above Ginny Mae's. In no time at all, they were laughing and splashing around, throwing handfuls of water in the air to watch the sun catch the droplets on the way back down.

While Delilah began sketching, Paul kept an eye on the girls. When his stomach rumbled, she looked up and quirked a brow. "Hungry?"

"I don't suppose you'd believe me if I said no." He grinned back at her.

"Polly! Ginny Mae! Come on back here. It's lunchtime!" She began pulling sandwiches and apples from the basket while the girls climbed out of the pool and raced each other to the blanket. Paul used the edges of the quilt to dry their legs. Soon they were all munching happily, enjoying the shady quiet.

"I like it here," Polly pronounced. "This is the bestest picnic ever."

"I think so, too." Delilah mopped crumbs off of Ginny's face. "But now I think it's time for a little rest."

"I'm not sleepy," Polly protested, utterly sincere after a satisfying yawn.

"Me, too." Ginny Mae's eyelids drooped as Delilah tucked them both in the quilt.

"Then you'll be awake and playing again before you know it," Paul consoled. In a matter of minutes, the two children were fast asleep, light eyelashes dusting rosy cheeks.

"They're so sweet." Delilah tenderly tucked a stray hair behind Polly's ear.

"Sure are. Best to let them sleep so they stay that way, though." Paul tilted his hat over his eyes and leaned against the tree trunk, breathing in the fresh scent of the grass and the moist earth.

Delilah propped up her sketchbook, and soon Paul heard the rasp of pencil on paper. Readjusting his hat, he watched her record every minute detail with tiny strokes and delicate shading. At last, she breathed a sigh of satisfaction and held the sketch at arm's length for a final viewing.

Paul could scarcely believe his eyes.

❧

"It's perfect." Paul spoke softly but startled Delilah nonetheless.

"Thank you." She made an expansive gesture. "But it doesn't do this justice."

"I disagree. You have a God-given talent, Delilah."

Ugh. Why is it that every time we start to talk, just when I most enjoy his company, he starts going off about God again?

"I get the impression you don't agree with me." Paul's droll comment made Delilah realize she was being rude.

"I don't know."

"Yes, you do. What're you thinking, Delilah?"

"Mama always told me: 'Delilah, if you don't have anything nice to say—' "

"Don't say anything at all?" Paul finished. She looked at him in astonishment.

"What kind of advice is that?" she asked incredulously. "If someone asks you a question, you can't just ignore them!"

"It's an old proverb. If you only have unpleasant things to say, some people think it best not to voice them." His forehead creased as he gazed back. "What were you taught? If you don't have anything nice to say. . ."

"Say something vague." Delilah jumped when he burst into laughter. "Hush! You'll wake the girls!"

He cast a glance at the snoozing bundle and sobered up a bit—his wide grin still bearing witness to his mirth.

"What's so funny, anyway?"

"Oh, I was just remembering how you dealt with the MacPherson brothers." He peered at her curiously. "You really do live by that rule, don't you?"

"To each her own." She shrugged.

"Aha! See, you just did it again. Not giving a real answer but being vague. Look at me." Paul waited until she stared into his blue eyes before speaking again. "You don't ever have to be vague with me. I want to know exactly how you feel and why you feel it."

"Can't I just try out your way and not say anything?" She gave a weak laugh.

"I never said it's my way—it's an old saying. I tell you what's on my mind, and I hope you feel comfortable enough with me to do the same."

His steady gaze told her he meant every word of it. She sighed and gave in. "I was thinking about how every time the two of us start talking, you always bring up God. Do you remember how I noticed it on our last picnic?"

"Of course I do." With anyone else, the words would have sounded defensive, but Paul remained utterly sincere. "Do you remember what I explained?"

"You said that God made everything beautiful, so whenever you admire something, you think of Him," she recited dully.

"So what's wrong?" He waited, obviously at a loss.

"I've been thinking about that ever since you said it," she began hesitantly, her words gathering strength as she finished. "And I think there's something you left out."

"What's that?"

"You say God created everything, right?" There was nothing she could do but walk him through it.

"Unto the heavens and the earth," he agreed.

"Then what about everything hurtful and ugly and mean? Why did He make those things if He loves us as much as you say?" She blurted out the questions, half-hoping Paul would have an answer but knowing the miserable truth that she was right.

He stayed silent for a long while.

"I should've just let it be. I'm sorry, Paul." She hated to have devastated something so much a part of who he was.

"I'm not. I'm just trying to think of how to put it into words. I stand by what I said—God created everything—but at the same time, the ugly things that cause pain weren't in His plan."

"How do you know? What other reason is there?"

"This is why I was thinking." He rubbed the back of his neck. "I hate to make a mess of explaining, but here goes: Everything God made was beautiful in the beginning, but evil has a way of turning things sour, taking something good and using it for the bad."

"So you're saying that God made the milk, but evil made it go sour?" She couldn't keep the scorn from her tone. "There are worse things than spoiled milk, Paul."

"I know. And I never said anything about milk. Take this example: Knives are incredibly useful tools—they help us cut meat, slice bread, shape leather, skin fish, whittle wood, and more. You even use yours to great effect for protection. These are all noble purposes for the blade, but it can also be used for harm.

"If you've ever read in the paper about someone being taken hostage, you know that a criminal can easily put that same knife to the throat of another human being to hurt or even kill. Either way, that's not why the knife was made, and it doesn't mean the blade itself is evil. Do you understand what I'm saying?"

"So you mean that we can all be tools for good or evil?"

"Exactly." Paul beamed, looking very satisfied with himself for explaining his point.

And I just don't have the heart to ask him my next question. Some things shouldn't be said, but I have to wonder, if we're tools, then who's using us?

fifteen

Delilah ignored the twinge in her arm and kept mixing flap-jack batter. Miriam and Alisa deserved to sleep late for once. Besides, she wanted to do something, anything, for the Chance family to show how much she appreciated their hospitality and generosity, and the entire Chance family had voted her down when she'd insisted on transferring the store credit Reba had paid her for the painting.

The twinge grew to a full-fledged ache, and Delilah realized she'd been taking her frustrations out on the batter. She set down the bowl and began ladling the goopy stuff onto the skillet, still somewhat amazed to see it become a soft, solid pancake.

The truth of the matter was, she'd finally found a home complete with friends and even family, but it hadn't turned out the way she'd planned.

I want a home and family of my own. She flipped a flapjack perfectly and smiled in satisfaction. *I've learned so much here that I'd make a good wife and mother. As long as I stay here, I'll just be kind of an extra without a say in family business.* Tears gathered in the corners of her eyes. Delilah wiped them away furiously and went after the last pancake.

Spluchh. The source of the disheartening squelch was one half-cooked flapjack now dangling from the ceiling. Delilah grabbed the mop, swiped the useless mess to the floor, and wiped up the sticky traces, then bent down to find the ornery little thing.

"Oh! Shortstack!" Delilah couldn't suppress a giggle as the kitten gave a mighty shake to dislodge the well-traveled pancake, then daintily trotted around it, sniffing and mewing plaintively.

"I know, that's not your breakfast." Delilah set down a saucer of cream. "Don't be so upset. You're just lucky it didn't land sticky side down on top of you. We'd never have gotten the batter out of your fur!"

"How much time have you been spending with Bryce?" Logan queried, obviously biting back a grin.

"As though you don't talk to your horse," Delilah shot back, knowing Logan shared Paul's fondness for his mount.

"All right, all right. You've got me." Everyone else wandered in and took their seats.

"Sure smells good." Titus eyed the platter with interest.

"Flapjacks, bacon, and coffee. Can't think of anything better." Paul slid onto the bench beside Delilah. Logan said grace, then began passing around the food.

"Miriam, looks like you outdid yourself this morning," Daniel praised, chopping Ginny Mae's breakfast into tiny bites.

"We didn't help." Alisa drizzled syrup on her plate. "Delilah made all this by herself." She stabbed a forkful and brought it to her lips, chewed for a moment, and proclaimed, "And it's absolutely wo—" Turning faintly green, she clapped her hands over her mouth and ran out of the room.

Titus shot after her an instant later, followed by Miriam, who grabbed a damp towel. Everyone else stared suspiciously at their plates.

"I don't understand," Delilah spluttered. "I know the recipe by heart." She frowned at the table, puzzled.

"I'm sure it's something else." Paul gallantly speared a bite and made as if to eat it when Delilah snatched it from his hand. Despite his bravado, even he seemed slightly relieved when Delilah swallowed with no apparent difficulty.

"They taste just fine to me." The door opened, and Miriam walked in, holding the damp towel to Alisa's forehead.

"Do you want to tell them?" Miriam tried to whisper, but her soft voice carried throughout the silent room. Alisa gave a faint shake of her head, apparently still not trusting herself to speak.

"That's just fine." Miriam patted Alisa's shoulder and looked around. "Titus didn't get back before we did?"

Just then, Titus banged the door and all but flew into the room. "I'm gonna be a daddy!" His smile could've lit the entire cabin, so brightly did his joy and pride shine.

After a chorus of congratulations, Miriam and Titus took a still-green Alisa back to her cabin to lie down for a bit.

"Hey! That means the food really is good!" At Bryce's comment, the men grabbed their forks and dug in with gusto.

ಶ

"I can't believe Reba's friend saw my painting and commissioned another one," Delilah exclaimed as they drove toward the fishing hole. "I'm so excited, I can scarce contain myself."

"You're a talented woman, Delilah. It doesn't surprise me at all." Paul watched with pleasure as Delilah expertly turned the horses around the last bend and brought them to a halt.

"Well done," he praised.

"Thanks to you." She smiled warmly as he helped her off the buckboard and they carried their supplies back to the fishing hole. "You're an excellent teacher, Paul."

Maybe in driving, but I haven't gotten the real lesson across yet. We've spent so much time together, and every moment I grow to love her more. Lord, why do I feel as though time is running out?

Miriam let me take the sling off the other day, and it won't be long at all before I'm back out on the ranch with the other men. I'll only see Delilah at meals or evening devotions. How do Gideon and Titus stand being away from Miriam and Alisa for so much of every day?

As soon as he'd asked the question, he knew the answer.

They knew their women would be waiting for them when they came back. Delilah liked it at Chance Ranch, but Paul could sense she didn't see it as a permanent home. Besides that, Gideon and Titus could look forward to eternity with their mates, but Delilah still didn't believe.

Lord, help me to reach her today. Please.

"It's amazing how different everything looks from just a few weeks ago." Delilah set up her sketchpad, and her pencil fairly flew across the page.

The light green of spring had given way to deeper, richer shades. Wildflowers peeked out from the fresh-scented grass. Birds no longer fluttered around scavenging for twigs but rather sat cozily in their egg-filled nests, unseen but trilling sweetly. The leaves on the trees had grown and filled out the branches, blocking more of the sunlight and adding an air of cool mystery.

In My time. The words rustled through the leaves in the breeze, and Paul knew he'd received his answer. Delilah might not accept the Lord today, but Paul needed to trust in his Creator's plan.

He bowed his head. *Lord, what of the desires of my heart? You know it's difficult for me to stand by. Forgive me for my doubts, Jesus. Give me words as Thou wouldst have me use them, and grant me patience to see them come to fruition. Give me strength to trust in Thy will. Amen.*

He'd been lost in his own thoughts for so long, Delilah had

finished her sketch and was peering at him, looking concerned.

"What's running through that head of yours, Paul?"

"How everything comes down to choices."

"True." She seemed to begin saying something but hesitated.

"I thought we agreed we weren't going be silent or vague," he gently teased.

"I wanted to say that that's one of the reasons I can't put my trust in your God." She spoke the words softly, seeming almost ashamed.

"When you give your life to the Lord, Delilah, He doesn't make your choices for you. That's why He gave mankind free will. It's why we have to choose to accept His love in the first place."

"And that's why some people choose to do harm to others?"

"Yes."

"Why would He even allow that to happen, then?" Her frustration showed in the way she clutched her pencil in her fist.

"If He just made us all to love Him immediately, it wouldn't be a choice. It wouldn't mean as much. Love has to be freely given, not forced."

She stayed silent for a while, mulling that over.

"So our choices are to take His love or go to hell? Seems to me like He's stacked the deck, Paul. Love Me or else—not much of a choice, is it?"

Oh, Father, how lost Delilah is! Help me to show her the way into Thy arms. She's been hurt and sees things so differently.

"That's not the way to look at it. The truth of the matter is we've all sinned and fallen short of the glory of God, so we deserve death. God sent His Son to be the sacrifice so that, if we choose to accept the magnitude of His love, we can live with Him forever and share His joy."

"How have you sinned?" She looked at him shrewdly.

"You're a good man."

"Every time I think a mean thought about another. Every time I shirked a chore to come to this fishing hole when I was young. Any time I said anything less than the honest truth. How we live day to day is filled with small choices. No one chooses the right thing every single time. The Lord doesn't call us to be perfect; He calls us to be the very best we can be. To look at ourselves and admit our faults and to actively try to be better."

"And if you make the wrong choice?"

"You repent, ask for forgiveness, and learn from the mistake."

"So even after you accept Christ, you still mess up and make the wrong choices, and you still go forward?"

"Exactly. Choosing God isn't a one-time decision. It's a decision we make every time we have a choice. And if we mess up, His grace continues to cover us. He promises to be with us always. God never turns His back on us—we're the ones who turn our backs on Him."

"It sounds like so much responsibility." She looked as though a heavy weight had settled on her shoulders.

"That's why God is there to carry us through. You have the assurance to know you never face anything alone. You just have to decide to choose His love and grace over your own independence."

She silently gathered up her supplies, and he followed her to the wagon. Neither of them said a word on the drive home. Paul prayed earnestly the entire way, knowing she battled her thoughts and doubts.

"I can't do it, Paul." She stood in the barn after taking care of Speck. "It is *my* choice, right? Please don't be too disappointed." Her amber eyes glowed with distress, pleading with him.

"I can't help being disappointed, Delilah." His voice

sounded gruff even to his own ears. "I don't want to lose you."

"Listen to me." Her jaw set. "If you're talking about after we die and all of that, I have to tell you that I've seen death claim a person I loved. Nothing is more final. They've gone and you can't follow them. There's nothing left of who they used to be." Her voice cracked, and he put his arms around her.

"It's not just that, Delilah, although that's very important to me." He took a deep breath and said what had to be said. "The Bible tells us we can't be unequally yoked."

"What does that mean?"

"A believer cannot wed a nonbeliever."

She pulled away from him as though his touch burned her.

"Delilah, please understand what I'm saying."

"Oh, I understand perfectly," she spat bitterly. "I'm not good enough for you the way I am, and your loving God who allows you any choice you please won't let you accept me." Tears sparkled in her golden eyes as she whirled and fled to her cabin. Even from the barn, he heard the door slam.

sixteen

With a heavy heart, Paul plodded to the kitchen. *Lord, why does it have to be this way? This is too hard.*

Miriam took one look at his face when he entered the kitchen and shooed him into the parlor and onto the sofa.

"What happened?"

He poured out the entire exchange, desperate for any advice she could give him. When he finished, she asked quietly, "Paul, you put a lot on the table today. Now you've got to give her enough time to take it all in."

"I didn't handle it very well, did I?" He buried his face in his hands.

"You'll have to trust that the Lord knows how best to reach her. You've been seeking His will and asked Him to speak through you. Only He knows what it'll take to break through that wall around her heart. He's been tapping."

Paul let loose a heavy sigh. "It hasn't worked. If you ask me, it's about time He gave it a good knock."

❧

As much as Delilah tried to ignore it, the knocking wouldn't stop. It seemed as though Paul were determined to break down her door.

"I said, 'Go away, Paul!'" She buried her face back in the pillow to muffle her crying.

"It's Miriam, you goose. Now open up this door so we can talk."

Grudgingly, Delilah got up, threw the bolt, and cracked

the door open. After peering around to make sure Paul wasn't lurking anywhere nearby, she pulled her cousin inside and locked the door again before sinking back down on the bed.

"If you want to know what happened, you should talk to your brother-in-law." Delilah heard the bitterness spewing from her mouth but couldn't stop it. The pain poured straight from her heart.

"I already did." Miriam sat down beside her, put an arm around her shoulders, and tucked Delilah close.

"So he told you about being 'unequally yoked'?" Her voice sounded tiny and far away.

Miriam nodded. "Yes. I knew it would come down to this, though. Chance men don't consider marriage lightly." Her cousin tried to look at the bright side, but Delilah would have none of it.

"He's not thinking about marrying me—he's thinking about not marrying me!" She ended on a wail and cried into Miriam's shoulder.

When the sobs led into a case of distressed hiccups, Miriam spoke again. "You know very well that wasn't what I meant."

"But—*hic*—it's true—*hic*—and you know—*hic*—it!"

"Let me see, now. The man told you he doesn't want to lose you and is disturbed by the thought that he can't marry you. Sounds to me as though he cares for you. Deeply."

Delilah drew a shuddering breath. "I feel the same way about him; that's why it hurts."

"Just so long as you're clear on what he tried to tell you."

"Most of it. I'm just not ready to give my life to God yet," Delilah bemoaned.

"Let me ask you something." Miriam looked at her intently. "If Paul asked you, would you marry him?"

Delilah took a minute to really think about that. Could she

trust him with her life? "Yes."

"But you know he's given his life to God, right?"

"Um-hm," she mumbled.

"So if you give Paul your hand, you're trusting it to God in a way, aren't you?"

"I never thought about it that way."

"Well, Paul is a man of the Lord. It's just as much a part of who he is as his brown hair. So at least some part of you already trusts God." Miriam patted her shoulder one more time and got to her feet. "I'm going to leave you to your thoughts. I already told Paul you'd be needing some time, so take as long as you need."

Miriam kissed Delilah's forehead, gave her one last hug, and toddled out of the room, hand resting fondly on her enlarged tummy.

Delilah did some quick calculations. It would be six weeks before Caleb came into the world. By then, Alisa would be pretty far into her pregnancy.

And where will I be?

❧

"San Francisco?" Paul repeated dumbly, unwilling to believe what Reba told him. He ignored the racket of the guests around the barn to listen closely

"That's right." The older woman smiled smugly. "I thought it might be good to mention it to you before I passed the message along to her. You're sweet on little Delilah, aren't you?" She took his silence for the affirmation she sought. "Have you told her yet?"

Paul grimaced, remembering the week before. He and Delilah had hardly spoken since then, and his nerves were stretched tighter than a rope around a bucking bull's neck. Still, he knew he had to respect the distance she kept. Until she spoke to him, he'd told himself to be content with sitting by her during supper and working himself into exhaustion on the ranch. It was the only way he could sleep these days.

"Botched it that bad, eh?" Reba winced. "Seems to me you'd best mend your fences before she deserts them altogether."

"Your friend and her husband are serious about setting her up in a studio in San Francisco?"

"That's right. They own a gallery back there and think they'd do well to feature Delilah's art. So, are you going to go and clear up those muddy waters, or are you going to watch them wash under the bridge and off to San Francisco?"

In My time. The refrain that had haunted him all week whispered in his ear once again.

But I've waited, Lord. I've tried to be patient! What if she doesn't speak to me before she goes? What if I just asked Reba not to tell her?

" 'Trust in the Lord with all thine heart, and lean not unto thine own understanding,' " Polly's tiny voice piped out happily a few yards away.

I get the message, Paul grudgingly conceded.

"Are these people decent folk, Reba? Can we trust them with one of our own?"

"As surely as I stand here today," Reba vowed.

"Then it's up to Delilah." He abruptly turned from Reba and headed for the barn, cutting through the throng of neighbors yacking about anything and everything.

❧

"Psst!"

Delilah looked around to see where the whisper came from. Hezzy gestured wildly from behind the corner of the barn. Obie stuck out his arm, holding a letter clutched in a massive fist with a grin beaming from ear to ear.

Delilah set down the empty pitcher and made her way as inconspicuously as possible. It seemed as though the women had written back to their beaus, and judging from those scruffy smiles, the news was good.

"So they wrote back?" she whispered, respecting their obvious wish to keep their neighbors in the dark for now.

"Yep. Looky 'ere, Miz Delilah." Obie thrust the much-creased sheaf into her hands. Delilah smoothed it and read:

Dear Mike,

You do me great honor in asking me to be your bride. God rest her soul, your mother knew your devotion each day of her sickness until God called her home. In those days, I learned of your tender heart and strong hands. I wanted to help you out in that sad time, and since you left, I've prayed God would bless you and your brothers. Hearing you are well made my heart leap, and when I read on and saw you were seeking a bride, I knew then and there 'twas every dream I ever had coming true.

Yes. Yes, yes, a million times yes. I'll come to Californy and marry you I'll work hard by your side, cook your meals, and bear your children.

I talked with Eunice and Lois. They're a-wanting to come along and marry up with your brothers, but their aunt is balking. She reared them from a young age, and she's been carrying on something fierce. My sister went calling on her. You know Lovejoy—she could reason a possum into a pie. It took some doing, but she managed.

You can tell Hezekiah and Obadiah that their intendeds will be coming, too.

None of the three of us has much to call her own, but we'll come with willing hearts and working hands. I'll be like Ruth in the Bible, going to a new place and getting married.

I pray God will bless us as He blessed her and Boaz.
                        With high hopes and a happy heart,
                                Temperance Spencer

"Oh, that's wonderful!" Delilah smiled and hugged each brother in turn.

"Mike's grabbin' Reba so's we cain send the money on the stage tomorra," Obie gushed.

Hezzie hooked his thumbs on his suspenders and all but strutted. "Cain you believe we's gonna get us some brides?"

"I couldn't be happier for you," Delilah assured them both. "When do you think they'll get here?"

"Near as Mike cain reckon, they'll be here afore winter. We cain't hardly wait." Obie stopped talking as they heard footsteps.

Mike, with Reba in tow, came around the corner. He plunged his hands into his pockets and thrust a fistful of cash at her. "So you'll send it tomorra?"

"First thing," Reba promised. "Congratulations, boys." She patiently listened to a lengthy recital of the Trevor sisters' charms before turning to Delilah.

"If you have a moment, we need to talk."

❧

Paul saddled Speck, vaulted on, and took off. He didn't really aim for anyplace in particular, just so long as he wouldn't have to be polite to anyone for a while. He had some questions to ask the Almighty.

Dozens of thoughts drummed around in his head, making his temples throb before he realized he'd wound up at the fishing hole. Loosely hitching Speck to a nearby tree, Paul headed over to the very place he and Delilah had gone earlier that week.

He could scarce believe that scant days ago he'd sat in this very shady knoll with Delilah, enjoying the beauty all around him and answering her questions about God. It was then he'd driven her away from them both.

"Lord, if she goes, a part of me goes with her." Silence met his announcement, and his shoulders slumped in defeat.

"Why didst Thou bring her here only to take her away? Why did I think she loved Chance Ranch as much as I do?" He paused. *Why did I think she loved me?*

seventeen

"Probably because Delilah does." Daniel's deep rumble came as a surprise to Paul.

"What are you doing here?"

"Don't know yet, but I figured you looked like you might do something stupid if nobody came after you."

"What are you blathering about?"

"Seems to me the last time you had your mind on that woman when you were riding, you broke your arm." Daniel plunked down on the grass beside him.

"I—" Paul's mouth snapped shut when he realized there was no denying the truth of his brother's assessment. He maintained a stubborn silence until curiosity got the better of him. "What do you mean, 'she does'?"

Daniel gave a heavy sigh. "Aside from maybe Miriam, have you ever seen a woman fix her mind so on helping out around here? She didn't know how to cook; she learned. She saw we didn't have a flower garden; she planted one. Polly and Ginny Mae yammer on about something or another she's done with 'em most every night before bed. And even I can see how much she likes this place just by the way she painted it." He made a broad, sweeping gesture.

"And that's what's got us into this mess in the first place," Paul grumbled, not certain whether Dan's estimation of Delilah made him feel better or worse.

"What makes you think she's leaving?"

"Reba's friends are offering to take Delilah back to San

Francisco with them, set her up in a fancy studio, and sell her paintings in their gallery."

"Still doesn't mean she's leaving."

"I haven't given her a reason to stay."

"So give her one."

"I can't. She's not a believer, Dan." Paul watched as Dan shook his head. "You just don't understand."

Dan's head jerked up, and he spoke fiercely. "Now you listen and listen good, Paul Chance, because I know a lot more than you understand. A good woman is a gift from God, someone who completes you and gives you joy." His voice almost cracked as he continued. "When you find that, you've got to hold on to it with both hands before He takes it away again. You have to fight for her with everything you are, or you'll lose her. You haven't got what it takes to go through life wondering if there was anything else you could've done. You don't have a reason to keep on going." Paul knew Dan spoke of his daughters.

"You don't really believe all that, Dan."

"More than anything else," he swore fervently.

"Then prove it," Paul challenged. "If Delilah and I do get married, you'll be the one to walk her down the aisle. None of this not attending the wedding."

Emotions warred on Dan's face. "All right," he spat out gruffly before he got to his feet and stomped away, leaving Paul to his thoughts once more.

When you find that, you've got to hold on to it with both hands before He takes it away again. Dan's words echoed in Paul's mind, resonating in his heart.

Lord, is she being taken away by Thee?

No response came.

Maybe I should listen to Dan and ask her to marry me. I've seen Thee stirring in her soul, and I know Thou wilt bring her to the fold.

Grim determination took hold of him. *She's my match, Lord! Thou knowest that! Why shouldn't I keep her for Thee?*

As soon as the thought crossed his mind, he knew the answer in his heart. *I wouldn't be keeping her for Thee. I'd be keeping her for myself.* Still, Paul straightened his shoulders, *we belong together as man and wife.*

"And two souls shall become one." The scripture Miriam had read at her wedding crossed his thoughts. He struggled to accept what his heart told him.

No. The Lord still holds my soul. I've already given it to Him. This way I'll just be bringing Delilah to Him, as well. Even as he reasoned his case, he knew the truth: A man and wife stood together as one in the eyes of God. If he married a nonbeliever, that could not be. He'd never find peace because he'd forever be torn between the Lord and his wife. That was no way to raise their children.

Lord, please let her stay. Help her to see Thy love and accept Thee so that I can take her as my bride. How can I choose between the two things most dear to me in the world?

Even as the prayer went up, Paul knew the awful truth. There had never been a choice.

❧

Delilah opened her folio and put in the watercolors she'd worked on this last week. The sheer number of them showed how hard she'd tried to keep her mind off Paul and her disappointment over how he hadn't spoken to her once since that awful day.

All the better. She blinked back another onslaught of tears at the thought of leaving him behind her. *At least I can remember Chance Ranch.*

She shut the folio and began pulling her clothes from the wall pegs, leaving aside the traveling set she'd worn when she first had arrived. Her heart clenched as she folded the forest green–colored day dress Alisa had given her, then altered for her.

I will have a studio of my own, she reminded herself. *A home where I can work on my paintings in peace without feeling dependent on anyone else. It's just what I've always wanted. I should be happy.*

Then why aren't you? a tiny piece of her heart demanded as she held the jewelry box Miriam had given her for her birthday.

Because I hoped Paul would ask me to stay, her heart cried, *but he didn't say a word.*

She glanced out the window, spying the tender green shoots of the garden they'd planted together. She gathered her resolve. *From the start, I've said I couldn't stay here forever.*

"I am happy." She spoke aloud, shooing away her doubts.

"I'm glad to hear that." Miriam and Alisa came through the doorway.

Not certain what to say, Delilah shot them a smile before opening the drawer on her washstand.

"I can't believe you're leaving this afternoon! It seems like you just got here." Alisa pulled Delilah into a spontaneous hug.

"Here. We finished it last night." Miriam held out a cloak made of the soft wool they'd bought from Reba not so long ago.

"We couldn't let you go traveling without it, even though it'll be summer soon." Alisa folded it up and laid it in Delilah's satchel.

Touched by their thoughtfulness, Delilah fought a fresh onslaught of tears.

The women helped her finish packing, and Delilah picked up her satchel. Noticing how much heavier it was than when she'd arrived, she walked up to the waiting buckboard. She gave one last look at the homestead and realized the weight of that valise couldn't compete with the heaviness of her heart.

&

Paul numbly watched as everyone at Chance Ranch said their good-byes to Delilah. When she reached him, he took her hand in his, looked into her golden eyes one last time. "May God be with you, Delilah." His final words were a fervent prayer, one last plea for her to change her mind about everything. About God. About being his wife. About leaving for San Francisco.

"Good-bye, Paul." Her voice caught. When she drew a shaky breath and tugged her hand out of his grasp, he knew he was letting her go. . .possibly forever. He tried to swallow the lump in his throat but couldn't speak as she climbed onto the buckboard and drove off.

Lord, I chose Thee. Now, what wilt Thou choose to do with each of us?

&

Six days later, Delilah let loose a sigh of relief as she unbuttoned her shoes and curled her toes for the first time all day. She stretched and smiled as Shortstack pounced on a tattered ball of yarn in the corner.

The Munroes had been as good as their word. Founders of the San Francisco Art Society a mere year before, they'd set her up in a clever little cottage and introduced her to the artisans of the city.

Today they'd unveiled her first display at their gallery, and she'd heard so much praise, her head felt as though it would burst. One thing was certain: She'd find no shortage of patrons here. As a matter of fact, she'd best get some sleep. Tomorrow she'd need to paint enough to replace the pictures sold today.

Shortstack curled up at her feet as Delilah snuggled into

bed only to find her mind too active for sleep just yet. This had been happening ever since she left Chance Ranch. In the short span of time she'd been in San Francisco, she'd found herself so restless, she'd been working rather than sleeping. Pushing aside the covers and ignoring an indignant meow from Shortstack as she scrambled out from under the pile, Delilah padded across the room and began lighting lamps. She passed by the small round mirror on the washstand and caught a glance of dark purple shadows under her eyes.

Well, I may not be getting my beauty rest, but at least I haven't been idle.

She sank her toes into the large braided rug she'd made over the last week and ran her palm over the quilted coverlet she'd begun with Miriam and Alisa but finished alone. She made her way toward the window, wanting some fresh air. Deciding against opening it at night in a town still too strange for comfort, she fingered the curtains she'd stitched and hung, trying to make the cottage her home.

These would be so charming in my cabin back at Chance Ranch. I always wanted to decorate with a splash of color. I would have loved to hang some of my landscapes on the wall. I'd put one right over the foldaway desk. She closed her eyes and imagined how different the cabin would seem with paintings resting against the freshly whitewashed walls, her first quilt cushioning the bed, and the sprigged curtains fluttering in the warm summer breeze while Shortstack batted the edges. *And if I looked out the window, I'd see the garden in full bloom.*

She shook the thought away. She had a new life now—a home of her own and independent means. She purposely strode over to her desk and picked up her sketchbook.

Settling into a nearby chair, she began flipping through the pages, setting aside those she thought would make the best paintings. The various landscapes of Chance Ranch tugged at her heart. There was the homestead as it stood when she left, her garden beginning to blossom. Here she'd given her imagination free rein, depicting lavish blossoms amid a sea of green.

Sorrow engulfed her as she set that one aside. Putting up that portrait for sale would be like selling her dreams. *Maybe I can go back someday to visit Miriam and see Caleb.* Somehow, that thought only made her more aware of how she'd be missing Caleb's birth.

What if something goes wrong, and I'm not there to help? Fear washed over her. *There's nothing I can do all the way out here.* She wanted to cry at the very thought of not being there for Miriam, who'd given her so much.

Paul always prayed. I could, too. For the first time, Delilah didn't push the thought away. What harm could come from it if she tried? At best, she'd gain God's blessings for her cousin and some comfort for herself. At worst, it wouldn't work and she'd feel just the same as she did now—helpless and alone.

She took a deep breath and plunged in. "Lord, I know I have no right to ask You for anything when I've denied You for so long. To be honest, I'm still not sure I can trust You, but I'm not asking this for myself. Please be with Miriam and Caleb while I can't. I'm not free to go to them."

The thought of Paul's stoic expression as she'd waved goodbye stung her deeply. How could she face him when he'd made it clear she hadn't made the choice he wanted her to?

I still can. Didn't I just pray? Doesn't that mean something? Plagued by her thoughts, Delilah pulled open her dresser. Surely if she began painting, she'd exhaust this restless energy. She reached into the drawer and saw her mother's Bible resting beside a folder of her very first sketches.

Maybe the answer won't come from my hands, Delilah realized. *There's no shame in admitting I might be wrong.* She picked up the Bible, her fingers sliding over the leather, worn smooth by her mother's hands.

Trembling, she clasped it to her, hugging it tight. She hadn't opened it since Mama died. Crawling back in bed, she laid it on the pillow beside her, letting it fall open.

" 'If we say that we have no sin, we deceive ourselves, and the truth is not in us,' " she read.

I never said I had no sin, Delilah protested, but her gaze stayed riveted to the page. The words seemed strangely familiar, and she remembered Paul quoting this passage the morning he'd broken his arm and taught her to gather eggs.

" 'If we confess our sins, he is faithful and just to forgive us our sins, and to cleanse us from all unrighteousness.' "

I haven't confessed them, she admitted. *But since I have sinned, even if I did repent, why would He be faithful and just to forgive me?*

Shortstack hopped onto the bed, reaching out a dainty paw to bat the frayed edge of the ribbon Mama used as a place-holder. Gently pushing the kitten away, Delilah flipped over to the bookmark and found a marked passage in John 3.

" 'For God so loved the world, that he gave his only begotten Son, that whosoever believeth in him should not perish, but have everlasting life.' "

I remember learning this when I was little. That's what was niggling in the back of my mind when Paul spoke about living forever! Excitement mounting, she kept reading.

" 'For God sent not his Son into the world to condemn the world; but that the world through him might be saved. He that believeth on him is not condemned: but he that believeth not is condemned already, because he hath not believed in the name of the only begotten Son of God.'"

That's me. This is what Paul was trying to tell me. Because I don't believe in God, I'm condemned. But I don't feel lost in despair because Mama died. She believed in this. And it's not too late for me to believe, too. But can I trust Him?

That thought brought her up cold, until she remembered what Miriam had pointed out. "If you give Paul your hand, in a way, you're trusting it to God."

"I do trust Paul. I trust him because he's not like Papa." For the first time, she allowed herself to make the comparison. "He won't put an insubstantial dream above my feelings."

But Paul put God before my feelings. The realization took her breath away and made her head whirl. *And I trust Him enough to put Miriam and Caleb in His hands. When did God stop being some vague notion and an important part of my life?*

When you let Me.

Tears trickled down Delilah's cheeks as she prayed long into the night, thanking God for His unfailing love and forgiveness and finally accepting her need of it.

eighteen

Paul corralled the last steer and walked Speck over to where Logan and Bryce rested on their mounts, deep in conversation.

"No question about it." Logan's somber pronouncement made Paul uneasy. "It has to be done."

"What has to be done?" The way the two of them jumped hardly offered any reassurance. "What're you two scheming now?"

"I'm calling a Chance vote, that's what." Logan's bravado wavered somewhat when he snuck a glance at Bryce for confirmation.

"About what?" Paul walked Speck a step closer, pleased that his younger brothers stood their ground but irritated nonetheless.

"You'll find out along with Gideon, Titus, and Daniel. There're on their way over now." Bryce pointed to three men on horseback.

Paul shifted in the saddle, anxious to find out what was afoot and suddenly eager to get back to work.

"What're y'all lollygagging around for?" Daniel grumped as soon as they all stood within earshot.

"Logan and Bryce. . . ," Paul jerked a thumb in their general direction, "are calling a Chance vote."

"About what?" Titus and Gideon seemed just as wary as Paul felt.

"Well," Logan straightened in the saddle, "no offense to Miriam and Alisa, who do their best around here, we know, but seems as though things around here are on the decline."

"Yep. We've gotten used to certain. . .comforts," Bryce interjected. "So basically, what we're saying is—"

"We want to eat good food again!" Logan abandoned any attempt to make their cause seem lofty.

"Miriam needs her rest." Gideon glowered at the upstarts. "She's due this month!"

"Aw, anyone can see she's 'bout ready to pop, Gideon," Bryce soothed. "We wasn't talkin' 'bout her."

"Well, Alisa hasn't been well, either," Titus groused.

"You don't get it," Logan grumbled. "We ain't complaining about your wives; we just have a solution. A way of making sure they're not overworked and we're not underfed."

"Oh, no, you don't," Paul barked as soon as he saw where this entire debacle was headed.

"Oh, yes, they do." Daniel's habitual scowl disappeared into a cheeky grin. "All in favor of bringing Delilah back?"

Only Speck backed up Paul's nay, and even that was more of an equine whinny than anything else.

"And we know how Miriam and Alisa would vote if they were here. Motion passed. Now, I vote Paul goes to fetch her." Daniel leaned back, pleased as punch to see Paul outvoted once again. "That settles it. You're going."

Less than an hour later, Paul sat on the buckboard, driving toward Delilah. *Lord, I have to say I have my doubts about this. I'm not sure if I can bring her back and not aim to keep her. Please give me strength to do Thy will. Please watch over my love.*

As he passed through town, he pulled up in front of the mercantile. He clomped toward the back, his heavy footsteps suiting his mood.

"Hello there, Paul. Let me just grab my bag, and we'll get

to Miriam straight away!" Reba bustled through the curtain before he could get a word out.

"Not yet, Reba!"

She poked her head out and peered at him. "No?"

"No. But Miriam sent this with me." He thrust a letter toward the older woman. "She said it might be her last chance to write her parents before the babe comes."

Reba clucked her tongue. "And to think you had me all riled. Couldn't it have waited until next Sunday?"

"Probably," Paul allowed, "but I was heading through, anyway."

"Where you headed?"

"San Francisco."

A knowing glint shone in Reba's eyes, and Paul hastened to correct her. "Miriam and Alisa need the help, that's all."

"Sure it is." Reba swapped him a handful of peppermint sticks for the letter. "For your trip."

Paul chuckled as he left the store, certain she'd intentionally given him peppermint rather than black licorice because she thought there might still be a future for him and Delilah.

Lord, I hope she's right.

❧

Delilah hummed happily, if a bit off-key, as she walked back to her studio from the Munroes' place.

The fledgling city bustled almost nonstop, from boots clicking on boardwalks to buildings being built, one could never escape the sounds. Since the establishment of the San Francisco Bar Association, businesses had sprung up seemingly overnight, relying on Joshua Norton's plan to bridge the bay between San Francisco and Oakland. As prosperous and energetic a place as this was, she would gladly trade it all to be sitting by the fishing hole at Chance Ranch.

Thank You, Lord! They still want my paintings even if I have to ship them from Chance Ranch. Now. . .

Her jaunty step slowed as she contemplated what she planned. *Please give me the courage to go back. I don't know if You will bring me and Paul together or not. If not, it'll break my heart.*

Fresh doubts flooded over her. *No, no, no! I am putting my faith in You, Lord! Even if I don't stay at Chance Ranch, the Munroes have been so kind as to assure me of a place here. Still, I do wish there were some way I could be sure I'm doing the right thing.*

She turned onto the walkway to her studio and halted when she saw someone peering into her window. Despite her instinct to leave immediately, something held her fast. Those broad, powerful shoulders, the brown hair curling beneath the brim of a well-worn hat—Delilah's heartbeat quickened.

"Paul?" He must have heard her hopeful whisper, because he froze, then turned to face her.

Oh, my. Lord, I just asked for a sign, and there's no questioning this has to be one, but his eyes are guarded. Why is he here?

ᶻ⋄

Sunlight framed Delilah, bathing her in gold and making her even more beautiful than he'd remembered. *Lord, she seems so serene, like she fits here. I see none of the sadness she bore when she left us. Is she finally happy, and I'm supposed to ask her to leave it all behind?*

He cleared his throat. "I need to talk with you for a minute."

"Come on in." Her warm smile sent tingles down his spine as he followed her into the charming structure. It resembled a cottage more than anything, but her easel stood by a large window next to a worktable.

With easy grace, she sank into an armchair by the small fireplace and gestured for him to do the same. She waited patiently for him to speak.

"I've come to bring you back to Chance Ranch." *Oh, well done, blurting it out like that. This was a mistake. Will she be disappointed I didn't come to fetch her as my bride? Even worse, will she be relieved?*

"I'll be ready to go in half an hour." He watched in amazement as she began tucking loose leaves of paper into her sketchbook and binding her folio. Dumbfounded, he walked over to explain. Didn't she want to know why? What if she misunderstood?

He held out a hand to stop her only to have her push art supplies at him.

"Why don't you go put these in the wagon while I pack my satchel?" She disappeared behind a partition, and he heard the rasp of a drawer opening.

Lord, what do I do? Dumping her things onto one of the armchairs, he strode over behind the partition only to be brought up cold. She'd dumped the contents of her drawer onto her bed. He gulped at the sight of delicate stockings and the corner of a white ruffled petticoat peeking out from under them.

Certain his ears were redder than ripe strawberries, he seized the only option left to him—retreat. He rushed back to the armchair, grabbed her art supplies, and didn't stop until he stood in the warm sunshine by the buckboard.

❧

Delilah stifled a giggle at the look on Paul's face as he fairly ran out of her studio; then she shoved her unmentionables into the valise. Well, no use crying over spilt milk. The bigger question was why he was taking her back.

Lord, I'm trying so hard to trust in You and in Paul, but I'm going to burst if I don't find out soon whether he came because he missed me or something else. He doesn't seem worried like he'd be if anybody was hurt back at the ranch. Give me patience, Father!

She finished packing as quickly as possible, looked around one last time, and hefted her satchel to the doorway, where Paul took it.

"Come here." She picked up a squirming Shortstack, grown far bigger than she'd been on Delilah's birthday, and tucked her into a large basket. Shortstack gave an indignant meow before settling in. The cat gave a lurch to pop her head up through one of the basket flaps. When she seemed content just to see what was around her, Delilah couldn't bring herself to shut the basket again.

As they began leaving town, Paul cleared his throat. "Do you need to talk with anyone—make arrangements so everything's fine when you come back?"

Refusing to be discouraged by that statement, Delilah shook her head. "It's all been taken care of. I left a note on the table." Taking a deep breath, she looked him in the eye. "Will I be coming back?"

"That's up to you. For now, Miriam's pretty much in bed until the baby comes, and Alisa's green around the gills every day until the afternoon, but they're both too stubborn to admit they need help. We took a Chance vote, and I came to fetch you."

Another Chance vote, Delilah mused. *And to think, once I wondered if one of those famous votes would let me stay at Chance Ranch.*

"But that's not unusual. Neither of them is ailing other than that?" She had to make sure.

"Nope."

Now what? Is he going to stay quiet all the way home, Lord? Will he not say more than the bare minimum the whole time I'm at Chance Ranch? Give me strength and wisdom, Lord!

nineteen

"I'm so glad to hear that." Delilah debated whether or not to continue. "I've kept Miriam and Alisa in my prayers."

"We all have."

Delilah knew the instant her words sank in. Paul whipped his head around to face her and brought Speck to a dead halt with one jerk on the reins.

"What did you just say?" His intense gaze searched her face hungrily, and she smiled to see how desperate he was to hear her say the words.

"I've prayed for you all." Her heart sang as his face lit up with wonder.

"You've accepted Christ?" His voice was low and gruff. When she nodded, he gathered her in his arms and held on tight. "Then He's answered my prayers, too. What changed your mind?"

"I sat in San Francisco, completely independent, with a home of my own and new friends, but it wasn't what I'd thought it would be. I wasn't at Chance Ranch anymore, so I had to trust God to take care of the people I love. It was so much easier than I'd thought, once I made the decision. And since then, I've remembered all the things you've told me about God's love, and I can see it all around me."

"Whatever is good and lovely cometh from the Lord." He cupped her chin in his palm. "Now do you know why I think of God so much when we're together?"

"No," she confessed, "but it doesn't make me jealous."

"It never detracted from our time together. I think of Him when you're near me because, to me, you're the loveliest thing He ever made. I love you, Delilah." His voice deepened as he took her hand in his.

"I love you, too," she whispered, raising a hand to stroke his cheek.

"Delilah, will you do me the honor of becoming my wife before God and man?"

"Yes." As his lips met hers, a warm rush tingled from her lips to her toes. Delilah rested in the circle of his arms, feeling more cherished than she'd have ever thought possible. "Let's go home."

※

"The second I saw you two holding hands, I knew we'd done right by you, Brother." Daniel clapped a hand on Paul's shoulder.

"Now, if that's not the sorriest excuse I've ever heard for your meddling, I don't know what is." Paul grinned to take the sting from his words. "Truth of the matter is, she'd just told Reba's friends she was coming back here, so don't get too cocky."

"Aw, I'm just ready for some of those flapjacks tomorrow. Now let's get to bed. The sooner we wake up, the sooner we'll be at the table."

"I'm all for that." Paul hung up his hat. "It'll bring us one day closer to the Sunday you walk Delilah to the altar."

Daniel's brows knit together as he scowled. "About that. . ."

"Oh, no, you don't. A man's word is his bond." Paul flopped onto the bed. "Besides, you should've seen Delilah's face when I told her you'd volunteered."

"Humph. Volunteered," Daniel grumbled but ventured one last question as he put out the light. "Made her happy?"

"You'd better believe it."

&

Delilah watched with satisfaction as everyone—including Alisa—polished their plates. *Lord, how light I feel due to Your grace. I sit here as a member of not one, but two families. I belong at Chance Ranch, but You claim me as Your daughter. Thank You so much.*

She cleared the table and shooed Miriam back to bed, where Polly and Ginny Mae followed.

Alisa sank down on the bench. "It's so good to have you back. It feels as though you never left."

"Oh, I don't know about that." Delilah smiled and handed her a glass of cool water. "But I'm glad to be here."

"You know. . ." Alisa cocked her head to the side and scrutinized Delilah. "You're right. You've changed over the past weeks—you seem so much happier. Anyone can see the Lord shining through you now."

Delilah laid a towel over a bowl of bread dough and turned when Polly and Ginny Mae tumbled into the room.

"Auntie Miri-Em!" Polly gasped, pointing to the bedroom.

"What's wrong with Auntie Miriam?" Alisa hurried over.

"She had," Ginny Mae lowered her voice to a confidential whisper, "an accident."

"I'll go help Miriam while the two of you keep an eye on Auntie Alisa, okay?" Delilah hurried off to find Miriam stripping covers off her bed.

"What's wrong?" Delilah hastened to her side.

"My water broke. The baby's coming." Miriam calmly finished stripping the bed and laid down freshly laundered but tattered old quilts. "Go and ring the dinner bell so Gideon'll know to fetch Reba."

Delilah raced back to the kitchen, clanged with all her

might, told Alisa the news, and went back to help Miriam change into an old flannel nightgown and get in bed.

For the next hour, Alisa kept Polly and Ginny Mae busy while the Chance men milled around anxiously, each one steadfastly refusing to leave the house.

It was obvious the memory of Hannah weighed on their minds, and when Delilah hustled in to boil water, Alisa's worry was evident.

Delilah took her aside for a moment. "Listen, the contractions are pretty close together, but she's in good spirits, and Reba will be here any minute. Why don't you pray for Miriam and Caleb?"

"I have been. I want to be with her." Daniel overheard Alisa's request and broke away from the pacing herd of men. "Go ahead. I can take care of my little Pollywog and Ginny Mae." He bent down and started tickling his girls while Alisa followed Delilah back to Miriam's cabin.

"How are you doing?" Alisa sank down on the bed beside Miriam and held her sister-in-law's hand through another contraction.

"Pretty good." Miriam gave a wan but convincing smile, and Alisa relaxed visibly.

Reba sailed into the room and got down to business. After a few minutes, she eyed Miriam suspiciously. "How long have you been having contractions?"

Miriam waited to reply, gasping through another set before answering. "About three hours."

"You're one of those rare women who get through it in hardly any time at all." From that moment, there was no room for chitchat, and scarcely an hour later, Delilah handed Reba the twine and scissors to tie and sever the umbilical cord.

Delilah held a squirmy, slippery red baby and walked over to the basin of warm water to bathe the squalling infant. His little face screwed up as he wailed indignantly, and the only sound able to rival his lusty lungs were the happy shouts of his papa and uncles as Alisa told them mother and son were just fine.

Delilah wrapped Caleb in a blanket and walked over to the bed, where an exhausted Miriam smiled beatifically and reached out to hold her son.

She nuzzled her cheek against the soft duck fluff covering Caleb's head as Gideon strode into the room, tears of happiness filling his eyes at the sight of his wife and boy.

"Praise God," he got out hoarsely as he put an arm around Miriam's shoulders.

Delilah couldn't have agreed more.

❧

"You may not have heard the news yet," Gideon announced, beaming at the congregation. "But that's my son, Caleb, in my beautiful wife's arms, so on next Sunday, we're going to have a christening."

Whoops and cheers from the crowd drowned out anything more Gideon said as the men whistled and stomped their approval over the first boy born in Reliable. When things calmed down a bit, Gideon raised an arm and continued.

"And that's not all, folks. We have another special occasion that fine day. I'm pleased to announce the marriage of my brother Paul to Delilah Chadwick will also be taking place."

A hush fell over the crowd before ominous rumblings began. Hats moved back and forth as men shook their heads. Paul stood up next to Gideon.

"Everyone's invited." It did no good. Paul looked out at the sea of faces and saw set jaws, menacing scowls, and knuckles cracking.

Elias Scudd jumped to his feet. "Oh, no ya don't, Paul Chance." He jerked a thumb toward Delilah. "This un's spoken for."

Paul crossed his arms over his chest. "Yes, she is. By me."

"That ain't what he meant, and you know it!" Ross Dorsey yelled near the back rows.

"Why don't you explain it to me." Paul refused to lose his good humor. In all honesty, he couldn't blame the menfolk for being put out with him. "Who's spoken for her?"

In an instant, benches crashed to the ground as the men of Reliable jumped up to stand their ground. Every male on the premises let loose a resounding, "Me!"

"She can only have one husband," Reba managed to choke out before she burst out laughing.

"We know!"

"Just so long as his last name ain't Chance," Rusty growled as the crowd rumbled agreement.

"We done told ya from the first that was the way it had to be," Elias Scudd shouted.

"Yeah!"

"Sure as shootin'!"

Ross Dorsey shook a fist. "You greedy gophers already got two fine wimmen to care for ya!"

"Leave somethin' for the rest of us!" Rusty roared as the men became more worked up by the minute.

"She's ain't a flapjack, fellas!" Obie, Hezzy, and Mike waded to the front. "Ya cain't go claimin' her like that."

"Sure we can!" someone shouted back.

"No, ya cain't. Ya hafta treat a woman proper. Now, if Miz Delilah wants ta marry up with Paul here—" Hezzy clapped Paul's shoulder so hard his knees just about buckled "—you'll hafta git your own brides." Obie glowered from under bushy brows.

"Whatsa matter with you MacPhersons? None of y'all have a bride, neither!" Scudd glared right back.

"Sure we do." Mike stepped forward when Scudd scoffed at him.

"Yeah, right. How come nobody's seen 'em?" Rusty challenged.

"They'll be here afore winter." Hezzy rocked back on his heels.

Stunned, the men stayed silent for a heartbeat. Then someone offered a tentative, "How'd ya manage that?"

"Like I said, ya gotta court a fine woman, gentlemen. We wrote to 'em and asked 'em ta come down."

"Yee-haw! More women are on the way!" Everyone got riled up again at that realization.

"Now, see here," Obie barked. "Temperance, Eunice, and Lois are taken. Don't you be thinkin' they's fair game."

Groans filled the air. "Aw, come on!"

Paul decided this had gone on long enough. "If you left sweethearts back home, I say you should write to them. Travel a bit—find the woman who makes you happy. But I've already found mine, and I don't want to hear another word about it."

The throng parted when Delilah swept past the overturned benches to stand beside Paul. "I know you're all fine men, and I'd be honored to marry any one of you."

Elias Scudd preened at that comment while Ross Dorsey smoothed his sideburns.

"But you see. . ." She laced her fingers through Paul's. "I've given my heart to Paul Chance. I had hoped you'd all come to our wedding and share our happiness."

Everyone stayed silent for a stretch, the only sound the scuffling of boots in the dust as every man looked down, ashamed.

"Of course we will, Miz Delilah!" Rusty promised from the back.

Amid a flurry of "of course we wills," Delilah stood up on her tiptoes to plant a soft kiss on Paul's cheek. Life had never been better.

Delilah peeked out from behind the barn door and felt her heart might burst from fullness. Paul stood at a makeshift altar, dressed in his Sunday best and looking like the most handsome man on earth. The benches fairly groaned as everyone in Reliable settled in.

Miriam cuddled Caleb in her arms while Gideon held her. Logan and Bryce sat near the end, holding a place for the girls. Titus began singing "Blest Be the Tie That Binds" as he and Alisa marched down the aisle of benches to take their respective positions of best man and matron of honor. Polly carried a basket and strewed petals from their garden as she passed, grabbing handfuls and dropping them in tiny clumps. Ginny Mae toddled after her, carting along a patient Shortstack in a stranglehold until they reached their bench and plopped down in front of Reba and Gus.

All of these people had come to Delilah's wedding because they cared for her. *Thank You, Lord. You have blessed me beyond my biggest hopes.*

"Ready?" Daniel offered her his arm and a rare smile as she gave her golden dress one last brush.

Delilah dimly realized that everyone got to their feet as she came into view, but she kept her gaze fixed on Paul and his smile, full of love and warm promise. She was a gambler's daughter and had sworn not to follow in her father's footsteps. But here she stood with everyone she loved, taking a Chance who would change her entire life. She'd come home at last.

A Letter To Our Readers

Dear Reader:

In order that we might better contribute to your reading enjoyment, we would appreciate your taking a few minutes to respond to the following questions. We welcome your comments and read each form and letter we receive. When completed, please return to the following:

Fiction Editor
Heartsong Presents
PO Box 719
Uhrichsville, Ohio 44683

1. Did you enjoy reading *Taking a Chance* by Kelly Eileen Hake?
   ❏ Very much! I would like to see more books by this author!
   ❏ Moderately. I would have enjoyed it more if

   _____

   _____

   _____

2. Are you a member of **Heartsong Presents**? ❏ Yes ❏ No
   If no, where did you purchase this book? _____

   _____

3. How would you rate, on a scale from 1 (poor) to 5 (superior), the cover design? _____

4. On a scale from 1 (poor) to 10 (superior), please rate the following elements.

   ____ Heroine   ____ Plot
   ____ Hero   ____ Inspirational theme
   ____ Setting   ____ Secondary characters

5. These characters were special because? _____
_____.
_____.

6. How has this book inspired your life? _____
_____
_____

7. What settings would you like to see covered in future
   Heartsong Presents books? _____
_____
_____

8. What are some inspirational themes you would like to see
   treated in future books? _____
_____
_____

9. Would you be interested in reading other **Heartsong
   Presents** titles? ❏ Yes ❏ No

10. Please check your age range:
   ❏ Under 18   ❏ 18-24
   ❏ 25-34   ❏ 35-45
   ❏ 46-55   ❏ Over 55

Name _____
Occupation _____
Address _____

Virginia

4 stories in 1

Spanning the innocent age of tall ships through the victory of WWI, this captivating family saga celebrates the rich heritage of Virginia through four romance stories by author Cathy Marie Hake.

Innocence and intrigue, heartbreak and hope mingle in a world where God's grace and the power of love transform lives.

Historical, paperback, 464 pages, 5 ³/₁₆" x 8"

Presents

Great Inspirational Romance at a Great Price!

Heartsong Presents books are inspirational romances in contemporary and historical settings, designed to give you an enjoyable, spirit-lifting reading experience. You can choose wonderfully written titles from some of today's best authors like Peggy Darty, Sally Laity, DiAnn Mills, Colleen L. Reece, Debra White Smith, and many others.

When ordering quantities less than twelve, above titles are $2.97 each.
Not all titles may be available at time of order.

HEARTSONG
PRESENTS

If you love Christian romance…

$10.⁹⁹

You'll love Heartsong Presents' inspiring and faith-filled romances by today's very best Christian authors…DiAnn Mills, Wanda E. Brunstetter, and Yvonne Lehman, to mention a few!

When you join Heartsong Presents, you'll enjoy 4 brand-new mass market, 176-page books—two contemporary and two historical—that will build you up in your faith when you discover God's role in every relationship you read about!

Imagine…four new romances every four weeks—with men and women like you who long to meet the one God has chosen as the love of their lives…all for the low price of $10.99 postpaid.

To join, simply visit www.heartsong presents.com or complete the coupon below and mail it to the address provided.

Mass Market 176 Pages

YES! Sign me up for Heartsong!

NEW MEMBERSHIPS WILL BE SHIPPED IMMEDIATELY! Send no money now. We'll bill you only $10.99 post-paid with your first shipment of four books. Or for faster action, call 1-740-922-7280.

NAME _____

ADDRESS _____

CITY _____ STATE _____ ZIP _____

MAIL TO: HEARTSONG PRESENTS, P.O. Box 721, Uhrichsville, Ohio 44683 or sign up at WWW.HEARTSONGPRESENTS.COM

ADPG05